Beyond Borders

BEYOND BORDERS

An Anthology of New Writing from Manitoba,
Minnesota, Saskatchewan and the Dakotas

✦ ✦ ✦

Mark Vinz and
Dave Williamson, editors

NEW RIVERS PRESS / TURNSTONE PRESS

The publishers wish to express their gratitude to the following organizations who have contributed to the publication of this book: The North Dakota Council on the Arts, The South Dakota Arts Council, The National Endowment for the Arts (with funds appropriated by the Congress of the United States), The First Bank System Foundation, The Arts Development Fund of The United Arts Council, Liberty State Bank, The Tennant Company Foundation, The Manitoba Arts Council and The Canada Council.

 This activity is supported in part by a grant from the North Dakota Council on the Arts, an agency of the State of North Dakota.

NORTH DAKOTA COUNCIL ON THE ARTS

 SOUTH DAKOTA ARTS COUNCIL support is provided with funds from the State Legislature and the National Endowment for the Arts

Supported by the United Arts Fund

·U N I T E D   A R T S·

Cover art: Timothy Ray, courtesy Brian Melnychenko Gallery, Winnipeg
Text design: Marilyn Morton

U.S. ISBN 0-89823-146-9
Library of Congress Catalog Card Number 92-60178

Canadian Cataloguing in Publication Data

Main entry under title:

Beyond Borders

   ISBN 0-88801-165-2

1. Canadian literature (English) - Manitoba - 20th century.* 2. Canadian literature (English) - Saskatchewan - 20th century.* 3. American literature - North Dakota - 20th century. 4. American literature - South Dakota - 20th century. 5. American literature - Minnesota - 20th century. I. Vinz, Mark, 1942- II. Williamson, David, 1934-

PS8255.P7B49 1992   C810.809712   C92-098020-1
PR9198.2.P72B49 1992

Beyond Borders has been co-published by New Rivers Press, 420 North 5th St., Minneapolis, MN 55401, and Turnstone Press, 607-100 Arthur St., Winnipeg, Manitoba R3B 1H3, Canada, in a first edition of 2700 copies.

Contents

The Road Taken
A Two-Part Introduction

From the North

It was June, 1981, and the "Writing Across the Curriculum" movement was spreading across the United States. At Moorhead State University, it took the form of the Prairie Writing Project, with Keith Tandy at the helm. Anxious to find out more about it, I went down to Moorhead for a week-long workshop. Through discussion, individual assignments, lectures and four-person critique groups, we absorbed the principle that "if you can write it, you've learned it," and we found out how to apply this in all disciplines, not just English classes.

Tuesday evening was set aside for socializing. The plan was that each of the project faculty members would host a few of the workshop participants at his or her home. Having known the group of twenty-five for a whole two days, Tandy took it upon himself to bring kindred spirits together. For better or worse, he assigned me to the home of Mark Vinz.

That was the beginning of a series of visits—my family and I to Fargo-Moorhead, Mark and his family to Winnipeg. Mark introduced me to two a.m. breakfasts at places like the Fryn' Pan; I introduced him to two a.m. burgers at Salisbury House. What I had a hard time matching, though, was the Empire Bar in Fargo. Not only was the Empire what Canadians might call a "typical American bar," the beer was ridiculously inexpensive and on any given night you might get a handful of fishing lures free with every purchase. To add to the local color provided by the Empire staff and patrons, Mark could be counted on to include in our group one of his more interesting students or a newly imported poet like Thom Tammaro, or even someone who'd actually fought in Vietnam.

We'd sit in the uncomfortable booths of the old Empire and solve most of the world's problems. Mark would talk about his days as editor of *Dacotah Territory* and I'd talk about a truly Canadian phenomenon called the Manitoba Writers' Guild. We fantasized about ways in which we could get more north-south activity going in the writing community. The Canada Council had stimulated east-west activity in our country; it wasn't unusual for a writer to come to Manitoba from Newfoundland or British Columbia to give a reading. But what about the writers just two hundred miles south of us? Not only were they interesting, they seemed to be interested in *us*.

American interest in Canadian writing has never been better personified than by Rosemary Smith, a professor at Moorhead State and part of Tandy's Writing Project team. Rosemary called me a few years ago to tell me she was starting a Canadian Literature course and she wanted to know what novels she should read in preparation. I gave her my choices and suggested other people she should consult. Rosemary compiled a long list. She then proceeded to read *every* book on the list. Not only that—she took a year off and went to the University of New Brunswick to study Canadian literature. Rosemary has read more Can Lit than most Canadians.

I began to wonder: were the Americans more interested in us than we were in them?

I'd been reading American writers all my life, but mostly those who'd been published in New York. I knew almost nothing about the thousands of writers whose work mainly saw the light of day through American regional publishers or university quarterlies. Yet I was apparently seen by my Fargo-Moorhead friends as something of a curiosity: I was a Canadian who actually *liked* Americans.

Canadians continue to grapple with the problem of identity. Quebeckers cherish their language because they see that as the foundation of their culture. It is the most obvious element that makes them different from English Canada. But what distinguishes English-speaking Canadians from the rest of the continent? Too many people have defined Canadian culture in terms of their hatred for Americans.

Here then was a good reason for us to get to know one another better: we might discover that they weren't "ugly Americans" and they might see that we weren't wimpy cry-babies; we might discover that neither they nor we could be pigeon-holed under one national characteristic or another. We were individuals. And who better to foster this notion than writers?

Of course, we couldn't ignore the fact that they might like reading our stuff and we might like reading their stuff and we might spread the word about one another and prove that there's some mighty fine work being produced outside Toronto and New York.

So Mark invited a few of us to read at Moorhead State and we invited Rosemary Smith and Mark up to the Manitoba Writers' Guild conference. But, as pleasant as these jaunts were, we needed to broaden our scope. And as Mark's entrepreneurial friend, Joe Richardson, kept telling us at the Empire, it wasn't going to get done unless we did it. So we called the Saskatchewan Writers' Guild and asked if they wanted to get involved. And one Friday night in April 1988, Paul Wilson and Bonnie Burnard of Saskatchewan got together with Mark Vinz and Laurie Lam (then executive director of the Manitoba Guild) and me in a Winnipeg bar to talk about where and when the first major get-together should take place.

We thought that for the first event we should hold the line at twenty people. Mark knew of a monastery that might be the perfect venue. We'd invite five representatives from each of four regions: Minnesota, the Dakotas, Saskatchewan and Manitoba.

When the monastery idea fell through, Mark suggested an artist's retreat in northern Minnesota. He and Joe and I went there in early August to check it out—and also to fish in Rainy Lake. We caught lots of fish, but nowhere in the rustic buildings of Ober's Island could we find an appropriate meeting place. And so Mark decided he'd try to arrange for this all-important gathering to take place in Moorhead.

The Manitoba Arts Council was behind this venture all the way and so was the Saskatchewan Guild and, in October 1988, our dream started to come true. Nineteen people met all day Saturday at Moorhead State University, chatting about common concerns, voicing ideas on a large-scale conference and generally becoming acquainted with one another. The day was capped off by a reception at the Plains Art Museum, and it was there that the very first "gang reading" took place. The prospect of listening to fourteen writers read made even the most dedicated bibliophile shudder, but it worked! It worked because everybody respected the time allotment, and gang readings have become a highlight of every get-together since.

At the Moorhead meeting, Manitoba pledged to make this international initiative the theme of the Guild's annual conference in the fall of 1989. All the considerable energy of executive director Andrea Philp and her staff and of Ellen Smythe's conference committee was concentrated on making the conference a big success. It was going to be so big, it needed a March planning meeting, which we managed to tie in with the St. John's College conference and the Guild's annual general meeting. Six American writers and two Saskatchewan writers joined the usual Manitoba stalwarts for a meeting on Sunday morning and came up with a brilliant program with Robert Kroetsch and Carol Bly as keynote speakers. The theme was "Common Ground."

Meanwhile, Saskatchewan embarked on initiatives of its own, inviting Bill Holm and Linda Hasselstrom up for readings around the province (it was on that excursion that Bill discovered the musical streets of Mozart, Saskatchewan).

Common Ground was a roaring success and we vowed to perpetuate the idea. Birk Sproxton came from Alberta to observe and we encouraged him to get something going with Montana. Some people began to hint that an anthology might be a good way to validate what we were doing—a lasting souvenir but also a vehicle we could use for letting other parts of our two countries know about us.

In the fall of 1990, Mark organized another conference in Moorhead. It brought together more writers from the region and

introduced Bill Truesdale of Minneapolis's New Rivers Press to
David Arnason of Winnipeg's Turnstone Press. By then, the
anthology project was gaining momentum. New Rivers and
Turnstone would consider being co-publishers and Mark and I
were asked to make a concrete proposal.

In March 1991, the University of North Dakota devoted its
week-long 22nd Annual Writers' Conference to The Literatures of
Canada. Kicking off this prestigious event was a dinner at the
university and it warmed my heart to see all the Canadian flags
being used as center-pieces. Jay Meek and Bob King did a
marvelous job of organizing, making us feel like celebrities and
arranging comprehensive media coverage.

Within a couple of months, Mark and I were able to spread
the word: the anthology was going to be a reality. And, at the
same time, other people were making plans for carrying the
international initiative into the future: Regina in 1992, Bemidji
in 1993.

This anthology offers you a generous sampling of what we're
all about. In the comfort of your own home, you can relax with
twenty-four writers from the North American prairies, twenty-four
who believe that writing should know no boundaries.

Dave Williamson
Winnipeg, Manitoba

From the South

Occasionally, when I think about Dave Williamson and what
we've experienced together over the last ten years, I'm reminded
of one of Robert Frost's more famous poems, "The Road Not
Taken." It's a poem about making choices, about chance encounters, and about speculating in retrospect—what if? Well, I've done
a lot of that kind of speculating about the road that led to this

anthology, and about the education we've both received along the way.

Like most American readers (editors and writers, too, for that matter), I grew up knowing amazingly little about what was going on north of the border. Back in the days (1971-81) when I edited the poetry journal *Dacotah Territory*, I fancied myself as an importer-exporter: to send *out* the best writing from this region of the U.S. (i.e., the Upper Midwest); to bring *in* the best from anywhere, though for a long time we didn't receive any manuscripts from Canada. That began to change in 1973 when Grayce Ray (a Canadian native and citizen) became my associate editor. Grayce and her then-husband Tim introduced me to Robert Enright and I attended his eye-opening lecture on—and reading from—contemporary Canadian poetry. About that time I also began receiving copies of George Amabile's magazine *The Far Point* (later *Northern Light*) from Winnipeg, as well as copies of other Canadian literary magazines from Bill Tilland, an old friend from graduate school days who was teaching in Alberta and in the process of becoming a Canadian citizen. Another friend, William D. Elliott, began to talk about Canadian writers and scholars he had been discovering, and later to invite some of them to his university, Bemidji State. My education was certainly beginning, but it didn't take its most important turn until I met Dave Williamson a few years later.

Dave introduced me not only to Canadian books and magazines but to the writers themselves. As my acquaintance grew, so did my amazement at the world of good writing so close yet so far away. By that time I was no longer editing my magazine, but the old importer-exporter zeal survived, and now I had an ally, a friend, as interested in beginnings as I was. As I read the work of David Arnason and Di Brandt, Dennis Cooley and Carol Shields, to name but a few, I knew that these were writers Americans should know about—and it wasn't difficult to begin making commitments toward that end.

Since those years, those first visits to Winnipeg and the talks with writers and representatives of both the Manitoba and Saskatchewan writers' guilds, I've renewed my own commitments over and over again. Along the way, I've been struck with a number of things about writers at mid-continent, on either side of the border. First, there's an important commonality. The places which have shaped us are not all that different, and neither are some of our attitudes—such as the dedication to independent, decentralized publishing. The central plains and prairies are by and large regarded as simply *regional*, and whether it's by New York or Toronto, writers out here tend to be overlooked, taken for granted. That doesn't always show up in the writing, of course, but it's there, a kind of chip on the shoulder, and whether it results in a healthy or an ingrown skepticism, it's indeed something we have to deal with.

Aside from matters of individual styles and themes, there are some important differences, too. For one thing, I've found that Canadian writers are far more aware of contemporary literature in the U.S. than we are of its Canadian counterpart, far more aware, too, of contemporary literature in Europe. The university-based Canadian writers also seem far more attuned to current literary theory—modern vs. postmodern, for instance—and all the Canadian writers, no matter where they are based, are certainly better organized. The main difference is that brought about by the writers' guilds, within the province and beyond it, an ongoing network of writers, a support system for readings and publishing, book distribution and conferences. The unifying forces provided by provinces and by the Canada Council might be something for any U.S. writer to envy. We certainly don't have anything like it on this side of the border, not even within individual states.

These kinds of differences and similarities are certainly part of the ongoing fascination for north-south exploration, but what—in my own case, at least—overrides them all is the tremendous openness and generosity of spirit I've discovered in the vast majority of the individual writers I've come in contact with. This isn't the place to go into it, but I certainly understand why Canadians have every right to be frustrated with, even to loathe Americans. Suffice it to say that I've met with very few of those animosities. Free trade may remain a divisive issue internationally, but, as Bill Holm has said, perhaps the *real* free trade is what has motivated us as writers—what we've been able to stress is a common ground of attitude and spirit, what goes beyond borders, political or otherwise.

That has certainly been the aim of this anthology, at least of its co-editors. In it, Dave and I have wanted to involve those writers who've either been directly connected with the ongoing dialogue and exchanges, or those who've expressed strong interest in them, and who share the sense of exploration and education of which I've been writing. That has been reflected even in the titles we've considered. *Common Ground* is what we've called the phenomenon that has so captured us, though that title was taken by an anthology of poetry from the American Midwest that Thom Tammaro and I co-edited three years ago, and *Border Crossings*—an equally fitting title—had been used by Bob Enright to rechristen *Arts Manitoba Quarterly. Us and Them* was suggested (too separatist), *Free Trade* (too loaded), *From Plains to Prairies* or *Meeting at Midcontinent* (too regional), and *Border-lines* (too suggestive of "borderline," a connotation that certainly doesn't reflect the work we've read). After much discussion and many other suggestions, *Beyond Borders* finally seemed closest to what we were looking for, especially when coupled with a clear sense of region in a subtitle. While crossing borders has always been our aim, writing itself is always involved with borders, too—individually and collectively. In every sense, then, *Beyond Borders* represents a beginning.

Finally, I must add that choosing the individual work for the book has been a celebration—a renewing of old acquaintances and a discovery of new ones, and a renewing of admiration, too. Dave has maintained the most direct contact with the Canadian writers and with prose, I with the Americans and poetry. But there's nothing here that we haven't mutually discussed and agreed upon, and that certainly includes the editing of each other's work. Perhaps we should have left ourselves out of *Beyond Borders* except as editors, but that would be a little like abandoning a child we've worked hard to rear. Besides, we've wanted to be a part of things in every way possible. That's perhaps the most essential bond between the two of us. If we're both fascinated by beginnings, if we're both smitten with importer-exporter zeal, we're both a little afraid to miss out on things, too—and now, in retrospect, I'm indeed thankful for that particular shortcoming. Without it, perhaps neither of us would have been so willing to cross borders in the first place, to take the road that, as Robert Frost has said, "has made all the difference."

Mark Vinz
Moorhead, Minnesota

Beyond Borders

David Arnason

The Star Dollars

There was a girl once, born on the windswept prairie a few miles
south of Boissevain, whose father and mother had died, in the
way of fathers and mothers, the father drunk one night crashing
his skidoo into a municipal snowplow, the mother slowly dis-
emboweled by a doctor who gave her a hysterectomy, removed
a kidney, took out her gallbladder, removed her appendix until
finally he had hollowed her out completely. And the crops failed
as they do on the windswept prairie and the locusts came, and
hail and tornadoes, and long cold winters followed by drought
and sunscorched summers, so that the trees died and the grass
turned brown and the soil was blown from the fields. And in the
end the banker came, and the lawyers and the auctioneer and the
friends and the relatives until at last there was nothing left, not a
hoe nor a rake nor a shovel, not the doilies her mother had made
nor the silver spoons from Niagara Falls and Hamilton, not her
father's collection of pipes, nor his Ithaca Featherlight shotgun,
not her own Barbie doll nor the blue ribbon her calf had won at
the winter fair in Brandon. And so she had neither room to live
in nor bed to sleep in, neither roof nor floor, and she had only
the clothes she wore and a slice of bread the waitress at the cafe
at the Esso service station had given her. And when she was
forsaken, when she was bereft of all hope, when no one could
help her any more because they all had their own lives to lead,
she walked out into the fields of wheat and barley, into the fields
of flax and canola and rye. And of course she met a poor man,
she had always known she would, and when he cried for food
she gave him the entire slice of bread, because she was good and

generous, because when you are asked for a slice of bread it is hard to refuse even if you are hungry yourself. And she met a child, as she knew she would, the child cold and weeping, and she gave the child her bonnet to keep it warm. And the next child was also cold, all the children were cold, and she gave it her bodice to keep it warm, even as the third child claimed her blouse, and she had only a shift to keep the wind from her own body. And she came to a forest. Outside the town there is only field and forest, and if you walk through the field you must come to the forest, and she found a child there, at the entrance to the forest, a child weeping from the cold. She gave her shift to the child, and she walked naked into the forest saying to herself, "It is dark in the forest. No one can see me here." And she walked in the forest, naked in the darkness, and she knew that now she had nothing left, she had lost everything that she had ever had in the world. And as she walked, she realized that though she had nothing else, she had her nakedness. And as she ran her hands across her body, she realized that it was not a shameful nakedness. The stars above the forest poured down their light on her, and she prayed that they would shower her with dollars. But though she stood there a long time, they gave her nothing but their cold light. And after a while she became bolder in her nakedness, and in the morning she met a woodcutter who loved her for the bravery of her nakedness and he took her home and bought her a fancy dress and gave her food. But she refused the dress and took her confident nakedness to town, where the mayor offered to marry her and the banker offered to give her back the farm. But she refused them both and took her brilliant nakedness to the city, where she was toasted and cheered and offered great wealth. But she said no and she took her blinding nakedness to the capital, where princes vied for her hand, and she became a great star in the movies, and the dollars poured down from heaven onto her there where she stood.

Me and Alec Went Fishing with Rimbaud

Me and Alec went fishing with Rimbaud. Rimbaud was drunk. He was singing an old Hank Snow number, "Movin' On," but he had a terrible French accent, and he wasn't much of a singer. I was in the back of the boat, running the motor, and Alec was up front with Rimbaud. Rimbaud kept putting his hand on Alec's knee and calling him "my little pussycat," but Alec was too busy untying his fishing line to pay much attention. The motor kept catching fire, and I had to smother the flames with my nylon jacket.

Rimbaud and me were using pickerel rigs, but Alec ties his own flies. He makes lovely bluebottles out of black thread. He was dipping them into a little jar of garbage that he always carries with him because, he says, the fish like the smell. Rimbaud didn't like the smell, so he refused to sit with Alec. He wanted to sit in the back of the boat with me, but I didn't like the smell of Rimbaud, so I made him sit in the front. He got sulky and refused to talk, but a lot of nineteenth-century Frenchmen are like that, so I didn't worry too much.

We were drinking absinthe, passing around the bottle. You can't get absinthe in the local liquor store, but Alec's brother from Duluth had sent him a bottle. He'd been saving it for a special occasion, but it was his turn to bring the bottle and that's all he had in the house. Rimbaud got over his sulking fit pretty soon and was doing his imitation of Brenda Lee, only he got the words to "Jambalaya" mixed up with "Shrimp Boats Are A-Coming." He tried to kiss Alec on the neck, but Alec said, "Get away from me, you fag. Did you come out to fish or just to piss around?"

Rimbaud was miffed. "I'm a great tragic poet," he shouted. "I am red. See the laughter spill from my beautiful lips. Watch. I spit out blood. I don't have to take this treatment from you, you little turd."

He didn't actually spit blood, but it was pretty disgusting anyway. He'd been chewing Copenhagen, and he put a big brown gob on Alec's foot. Luckily, Alec didn't notice.

Now they were both sulking. The fish weren't biting anyway,

so I tried to cheer them up with a couple of Polish jokes, but it didn't work. They both claimed that they had Polish grandmothers, and said I'd affronted them. Rimbaud was trying to make up with Alec.

"You are green," he said, "a vibration of the divine seas, the peace of fresh meadows. Your great brow is furrowed with wrinkles."

"What do you mean, wrinkles?" Alec asked, a little testily.

"Well, you have to admit, you've got a lot of wrinkles."

"I do not."

"You do so."

"Do not."

"All right, forget it then. I was just trying to be friendly."

"Okay, but no more poetry. You're scaring the fish."

Rimbaud seemed to be satisfied with the new arrangement and he started humming "Jailhouse Rock." The motor caught fire again and I was a little worried. I'd burned up most of my nylon jacket already, and I wasn't sure there was enough left to smother the flames. I managed to get it out, though, and, when I turned around, Alec and Rimbaud were playing chess with a little magnetic chessboard that Rimbaud had in his pocket. They were quarreling again. Rimbaud accused Alec of stealing the white king.

"There was no white king, you silly bugger," Alec told him.

Rimbaud fixed Alec with a glacial stare. "Enough farting around, Alec," he said. "Let's be perfectly candid about this. You're jealous because I'm a great poet and you're just a little nobody, and so you've stolen my white king out of spite."

"Screw you."

Rimbaud leered. "That's a wonderful idea. But let's finish this game of chess first."

"It's finished," Alec said. "You've lost your king, so I win. That's the rules."

"That's not fair," Rimbaud shouted. "You've got to capture him."

"I did," Alec said, pulling the piece out of his shirt pocket. "I captured him while you were vomiting over the side of the boat." He passed the white king back to Rimbaud, who seemed a little bad-tempered about the whole business.

For a while everybody just fished. I caught a couple of saugers and Alec caught two perch and a sunfish. Rimbaud caught a tiny bullhead using a fly that Alec had given him, and he refused to throw it back. I told him they were no good to eat, but he said it looked sensitive, and he couldn't bear the thought of it having to live in that dirty water. Then he threw Alec's sunfish back because, he said, it was too ugly. Alec was pissed off because his father-in-law loves sunfish and he was going to give the fish to him. He refused to give Rimbaud any more flies, so Rimbaud had to use my minnows.

Rimbaud was singing an old Platters number, "The Great Pretender," and he was trying to do the backup stuff too. Alec asked me to make him stop, but he was Alec's friend, not mine. Besides, I was having trouble with the motor again. It's an old ten-horse Johnson with the gas tank built in, and you know how temperamental those things are. I took out the spark plug and dried it with a match. The motor chugged a couple of times and then finally started and I headed for shore because it had started to rain. Rimbaud and Alec were arguing again, but I couldn't make out what they were saying over the noise of the motor. Rimbaud had Alec's pocketknife and was threatening to commit suicide by driving it into his heart. Alec seemed to be telling him to go ahead. I screamed at them to sit down in the boat. Lake Winnipeg is dangerous enough without having a couple of poets fighting in your boat. Maybe I didn't tell you, but Alec is also a poet. Or at least he claims to be. He runs off his books on a little mimeograph machine he bought from the church when they got a Xerox. I can't make head nor tail of them. Anyway, that's how he met Rimbaud, at one of those poets' things.

When we got back to the dock, it was eleven o'clock, and Rimbaud wanted to go to the pub. I didn't think it was a good idea, because we were drunk enough. We'd finished the entire bottle of absinthe. Alec thought maybe we could pick up some women, but I told him I didn't want any woman you could pick up at the pub at eleven o'clock in the morning. Rimbaud didn't want any women either. He wanted Alec, but Alec told him to forget it. Rimbaud got sulky again, so we decided to go to the pub after all to cheer him up. When we got there, Rimbaud was singing "That's Amore," and doing a pretty good imitation of Dean Martin. I told him he'd have to stop because they don't allow singing in the pub. He said great poets could sing wherever they wanted. Alec threatened to break his fingers if he didn't stop. Alec and Rimbaud each ordered a mug of draft, and I had a Miller's High Life. You didn't used to be able to get it, and I wanted to see what it was like. It tasted pretty much the same as any other beer.

We had quite a few bottles and Alec and Rimbaud got into a big argument over poetry. Rimbaud claimed that the vowels were different colors, but Alec said that was just a figure of speech. Rimbaud claimed that he could actually see the colors and, by that time, he was so drunk, he probably could. I was thinking about Alice Simpson, who lives over in South Beach. Her husband left her with two little kids, and she's on welfare. She's really a good woman, but I figured, if I took over a bottle of gin, after a while maybe she wouldn't be so good. You know how it is when you get drunk. You get crazy ideas, but sometimes they work out.

Rimbaud had just moved over to Big Jim Maloney's table, and was telling Big Jim lies about all the fish we had caught. He had his hand on Big Jim's knee and was practically whispering in his ear. Big Jim didn't seem to mind, so you never can tell. Or maybe he's never met anyone like Rimbaud, so he didn't know what was going on. If that was the case, there was going to be hell to pay when Big Jim figured it out. Alec was muttering something, but when I asked him what he said, he told me he was singing an old Italian folk song that his mother had taught him.

I told Alec that I'd pick him up at five a.m. next Saturday to go fishing, but he couldn't bring any poets along. He said he'd promised some guy named D'Annuncio, but I said no way, no more poets. Painters or sculptors are fine because they keep their mouths shut, but poets are no good because they are always talking, and you lose your concentration and maybe you don't notice a nibble. Then I bought a mickey of gin and went to Alice Simpson's place and that worked out just fine.

Lamb's Lettuce

Rapunzel, Rapunzel, let down your hair. This is the cry of the witch. The witch wants only to preserve beauty and innocence. The mother's greed, the father's cowardice, these are the roots of the problem. Lamb's lettuce, the mother cries, I must have Lamb's.

What can a father do, there in the high-walled garden? He must give his unborn daughter to the witch. The child may not be a daughter, there may not be a birth, nothing is certain. What is the promise of an unborn daughter worth? A handful of Lamb's lettuce.

Later of course there is the high tower, the fair maiden combing her hair. Rapunzel, Rapunzel, let down your hair. This is the cry of the witch, her black rags flapping like a crow. And the golden hair tumbling from the window, spilling from the high window. The witch is up it in a minute, full of cautions, full of warnings for the fair maiden with the golden hair. The witch loves beauty and innocence. Who can blame her for wanting to preserve it? The maiden answers yes mother to the witch. She cannot know the shadowy negotiations of the past, her mother's greed, her father's cowardice.

Then must come the inevitable prince, son of the king, ravisher of maidens. The witch is out. She has gone on a journey. The prince in his slyness has listened from the forest. And what can we watchers do? The witch is too far away for us to call her. Rapunzel, Rapunzel, let down your hair, the king's son calls, and the innocent hair tumbles free. Now the prince is ascending, he enters the window, and we below can do nothing. What chance has Rapunzel against the smooth tongue of a prince? How can a young girl remember cautions when her guardians are absent?

When the witch returns, she understands in a moment. There is a knowing look in the eye of the girl. She has knowledge that is hard to come by in a lonely tower in the forest. The witch is maddened with rage, she is sick with grief. She cuts off Rapunzel's hair, a hopeless gesture. It will only grow again. She sends Rapunzel to a desert place. When the prince, despoiler of innocence, arrives again, she is ready. When he calls Rapunzel,

Rapunzel, let down your hair, the witch flings the hair out the window. When the prince reaches the window, she casts him to the ground, where his eyes are put out by the thorns on the bramble bush where he falls. Then the witch weeps for lost innocence, her black heart breaking for the beauty that has been tarnished, for the death that has entered the world. She is weeping still.

But that's not the end of the story. There is more to come. There are the seven years of wandering, Rapunzel with the twins, a boy and a girl, the fruit of her one mad hour. At last they meet again, Rapunzel and the prince. She weeps tears of joy, crystal tears which fall on the prince's eyelids, and he sees again. They return to his kingdom where they grow fat in a period of slow peace. The daughter is sold for a handful of Lamb's lettuce. The son becomes a famous ravisher of innocent maidens.

Ven Begamudré

Sand Dollars

When the children saw their first palm tree at Tampa Airport, they squealed like the three little pigs and made me take a picture of them reaching for its fronds. Vikas looked at it, stood there a long time soaking in the humidity, and shook his head. Later, after the children fell asleep without the usual "Aw, Mom, just this once?" he told me what bothered him. Not so much bothered. Niggled. He's been back to India a few times with his folks, but this is the first tropical place he's seen that's so developed, so refined. The second day he still kept an eye out for beggars and for cows grazing in the street and said even the palm trees look refined. When the girl at the condo, the recreation director, said the City manicured the trees, he laughed and said to me, "Welcome to Florida," but I'd already guessed he would say that.

It happens a lot now, guessing what the other person thinks. Janine calls it a symptom of easy love. She envies me so much, sometimes I feel like telling her everything, like that affair Vikas had when I was pregnant with Alma. Now when our anniversary rolls around, I look at him and wonder how we ever managed six or seven years, never mind thirteen, fourteen, but I wish someone could tell me why we've started guessing what the other person thinks. We haven't done that since before we got married. And it's because we're doing it again that I had to come down here, never mind how tacky you said it would be.

You were right about one thing, people are ready to sell you anything down here. Alma just had to buy a Florida Snowman. Know what that is? A plastic jar full of water with a top hat and two little eyes and a carrot-like nose, all floating on the bottom.

I think there's even a red plastic scarf. I thought of you when I
saw it, thought how you'd melt under the sun here. You belong
back home—sorry—you're getting so cold and distant. If I ever
did give in, I'd keep you as my winter lover, but that's not enough.
I'd start wishing you were softer, hoping you'd melt the way he
does. I used to hate it when he fell asleep afterwards, but now I
guess I'd think something was wrong if he didn't. Janine's right,
it is easy love, not like ours would be, the one we'd share like
tramps huddled under a bridge.

There's a bridge called the Skyway here, which swoops up
into the sky and down again, kept up by bright yellow cables.
Next to it's the old bridge with two separate spans, one for traffic
going each way. Problem is, the one going south ends halfway
because a ship rammed it. That's you, I'm afraid, my bridge to
nowhere. If you tried, you could be the other span, the one that
keeps going, skims the water on low wooden pilings, but even
that's too scary for me. You see why I leave the driving to him?
It's all these bridges. There's even one called the Gandy Bridge
from St. Petersburg to Tampa. There's a sign before it:

> LONG BRIDGE AHEAD
> DO NOT STOP FOR FLAT

I watch the water and try to ignore his knuckles turning pale while
people pass without signaling. I used to hate it when I saw how
unsure he could be about some things. Now I guess I'd think
something was wrong if he never had any doubts. At least as long
as I can pretend he's in control, I feel safe. It's true with you I
don't have to pretend, but sometimes I wish I did have to.
Sometimes I wish you weren't so damned sure of yourself. That's
why I wish you'd fly down here. Not to save me from the gilded
cage you pretend I'm in, but to see the real Florida. It's not at all
like you imagined, you just have to know how to look for things.

Take the bird sanctuary. It's called the Suncoast Seabird
Sanctuary, started by a man named Ralph Heath, Jr., after he found
a cormorant he called Maynard staggering down Gulf Boulevard
with a broken wing. We drove up and down Indian Shores looking

for the place till we nearly gave up. Then we got out and walked and found it hidden among the condos. It's mainly full of pelicans, permanently crippled, living out their lives in huge pens covered with chicken wire. There's a sign near the office:

EMERGENCY BIRD ADMISSIONS
RING BELL
WILD BIRDS ONLY
WE DO NOT TREAT PETS

If Janine were here, she'd say, "Guess that leaves you out." Meaning me, of course—they would take you. The children's favorite was the pen with a turkey vulture and a black vulture, because they were eating off plates of dead chicks. The girls kept going, "Eyuck!" but I had to drag them away to look at the scarlet ibis and the sandhill crane.

Or take the light. Vikas has a theory people paint their houses according to the colors around them. Or in reaction to them. All the buildings here are vibrant. Pink and green, even shimmery gray. Know where it comes from? The light in the sky and the water. You've never seen light like this—you have to keep your sunglasses on even when it's cloudy. And it's true what they say about the sun in the tropics—it really does just drop out of sight like that. Why everyone has to say it's really true, I don't know, as if it's just a trick.

The other evening we went shopping on the boardwalk at John's Pass and I heard a woman squeal, "Sand dollars!" All behind her stood shelves of real ones, but she stood there mooning over placemats and reading the legend of the sand dollar to her husband. There's a star for the manger and a bell to ring, and the five holes stand for the five wounds of Christ—a little one for each of the nails and one above the center for the spear. I'm as religious as the next person, but ask me what people see in sand dollars. I like pinks, those mirror-perfect shells we see back home only at gas stations. Thanks to her, I found myself fingering a pair of earrings for Alma, gold-plated sand dollars the size of little golden suns.

The girls both claim they saw him first: the man who danced farewell to the sun. There he was on the end of a pier in his white shorts and T-shirt just dancing away. He kept his feet rooted to one spot, so he wouldn't get slivers I guess, but from the ankles up he moved like a gyroscope, a little to the right, a little to the left, like a cobra following the hole in the chanter. Did you know they don't really follow the music? Just the hole. He flapped his arms slowly, held them out and swiveled his wrists till I was sure they were double, even triple jointed. Snapped his fingers and danced for the sun. Poor Janine would've drooled on her manicured toenails. He reminded me of you, maybe a few years older; then I saw him up close and he must've been fifty. If you look like that twenty years from now, I'll gladly walk away from it all even if that would remind me how much older I looked. Who am I kidding, though? You won't. A person can't age gracefully back home. They wither and wrinkle from the wind and the cold, and their eyes turn blue. Not a warm inviting blue like the gulf at sunset where it's deep. An icy blue, a blue you won't see down here except in ads.

I saw a great one the other day, on a billboard with a huge handgun pointing at these words:

MORE LOCAL NEWS
WLFN RADIO

Sickening, maybe, but it was also Florida, like the tollbooth signs on the Bee Line Expressway to Cape Canaveral:

WARNING—ROBBERY CHALLENGE AREA
WHEN CHALLENGED BY AN OFFICER
DROP YOUR WEAPON
RAISE YOUR HANDS
DO NOT MOVE

Kennedy Space Center's in a wildlife sanctuary of all things. It was Vikas who mentioned it, of course—it wasn't me. There we have the military hovering like vultures over the shuttle program because it'll help them with Star Wars, and here we have an armadillo scurrying away from traffic. Rockets and armadillos, that's Florida.

More than just flamingos and oranges, though there are lots of those. The first three days I made Vikas stop at every orange stand I saw, bought so many bags I could start my own grove. I even took pictures of houses with orange trees in their yards till this blimp in a muumuu yelled across the street, "Never seen an orange tree before? That's how they grow, dearie!" Then her husband came out wearing a Blue Jays cap. As for flamingos, the only real ones we saw were at Walt Disney World.

Oh yes we did that too. First the Magic Kingdom. They should put a statue of Happy the Dwarf in front, because that's how everybody feels. Happy the Dwarf. It must be the music everywhere you go, always zippity-do-dah. No blues here, no melancholy baby. These Disney people know their stuff. Once I even sat next to a flower bed and music exploded from the begonias like pollen.

Alma just loved 20,000 Leagues Under the Sea, that ride through the lagoon. She's read the book and seen the movie, but I never knew she had a thing for Captain Nemo, all that stuff about the visionary hunted by the armies of the world because he wouldn't share his inventions with them. Hildy's favorite was the Haunted Mansion. She loved the part where you look in the mirror and see this ghost leering next to you. Will's was the Country Bear Jamboree. He clapped along and hooted when they did John Denver's song "Country Boy," except this one ends, "Thank God I'm a country bear!" Vikas went for the Jungle Cruise of all things. Even bought a Styrofoam pith helmet at a kiosk called Bwana Bob's. It's almost as if he's forgotten he's Indian, something he can't do back home where people ask him things like, "So how do you manage winter?" and he says, "The first five years were tough. The last thirty have been a breeze."

Then we did Epcot Center, starting at the far end in the World Showcase, ten gorgeous pavilions around a man-made lake. Like Expo in Vancouver only better because these are permanent. The Canadian one looks like a scaled-down Bessborough Hotel or Chateau Laurier. Vikas pretended he was American and said loudly with a straight face, "Caynayda, thayt wheyre they geyt all thayt snow in suhmer?" and I slapped his elbow, but it kept me from laughing at the poor hostess. Turned out she was from Winnipeg. She must hear such dumb lines every day, but how could she say anything with him grinning like an Oakie from Muskogee?

The children saved Future World for last. Mickey Mouse may rule the Magic Kingdom, Donald Duck may keep trying harder because he's number two, but the darling of Future World is a pink lizard called Figment, short for Figment of the Imagination. Will just had to have a Figment hat because the girls both got Mickey Mouse caps. The hat has orange horns growing from the top and two huge yellow eyes in front, even nostrils on the pink peak or beak. When he lowers his chin, you can't see him, only this pink lizard face. He can't see where he's going, of course—people just laugh when he bumps into them. Vikas and I bought matching Spaceship Earth sweatshirts. He hasn't worn his yet, but he said he might under his lab coat.

It's almost as if he's a different man, as if I'm having an affair with my own husband down here. It's exactly what you keep offering, the novelty of waking up with someone new. He's left the old him back in Regina, the one who starts work at seven every morning, comes home at seven every night. I never told you this because I didn't want to sound as if I was looking for an excuse to give in, but I eat with the children, then sit with him while he eats and goes on about the day's appointments. It's his way of unwinding, talking about his patients. He calls the latest Madam X after the Lana Turner movie, one of his favorites.

Poor Madam X. I know more about her insides than she does. The week before we left, Vikas did a diagnostic D and C on her and a laparoscopy and a retrograde dye transit. He never pushes, but I can tell he wants her to go ahead with an operation to free her right ovary. He won't guarantee success past fifty/fifty, but he loves a challenge. It scares him sometimes how good he is, and he thinks he'll get even better. His favorite quote's become, "Chance benefits the prepared mind," but if his patients knew what I know, they'd never go under his knife. He says when he's clicking, when everything goes perfectly, his instruments talk to

him. His hands are there just to hold the tiny lasers. They help
him pretend he's in control more than when he had to nick and
snip and slice.

Can you see it now? How could I ever turn my back on a man
who believes in himself so much? A man who helps God bring
babies into the world. Oh I know you don't think the world is fit
to bring babies into, but face it, you like playing things safe. No
pun intended. I nearly did throw you out of the house because
you were sure I'd give in. You'll never believe how close you
came—it wasn't just a line when I said it was me I didn't trust.

That Janine. I can't remember how many times she asked me
after you'd been over, "So how's the leaky faucet?" or, "How's the
burned-out thermocouple?" and I said it was just business like I
really meant it, and she knew it still was. She must've known what
could happen though, because you replaced her thermocouple
too, didn't you? Except I'm not going to use you as an excuse the
way she did when she left what's-his-name. Besides, you said it
yourself. You're getting too good at playing the halfway house. If
I leave Vikas, I'll leave for myself, not for another man.

I guess I've finally said it. I don't know what would hurt me
more, if you shrugged and said, "Have it your way," or if you
begged me to cross that line just once, so I wouldn't spend the
rest of my life wondering how it would've been. Don't you see?
That's my problem. I'm never sure with you. At least with him I
know where we stand, even if it's far apart sometimes. Sure it's
easy love, but so what? I deserve something easy at long last.

Damn it, damn it, damn it. Yesterday I kept hoping you'd
turn up.

Once I even thought you did, disguised as a security guard.
When I said, "Excuse me," and he turned around, I had to say,
"I'm sorry, I thought you were someone else." He said, "Ah'm
sorra ah'm noat," and swaggered off as if he'd made my day. We
were in Sarasota. Vikas and the children spent hours in the circus
gallery with its old wagons and posters of clowns. I never realized
he always dreamed of running away to join the circus, or his
favorite movie when he was little was *Toby Tyler*, a Disney movie,
of course.

The Ringling House was great. More than rockets and armadillos, more than flamingos and oranges, that house is Florida in a nutshell. It's a hodgepodge, a mishmash of east and west built by a man with more money than taste. The windows are shaped like oriental doorways, with that fluted arch Vikas says he's only seen on Indian palaces, or sets for quaint French operas. The music room has paintings on the ceiling with dancers from different countries, and the women from India and somewhere else exotic have bare breasts. I guess that's the closest you could come to porn in the twenties or thirties. You couldn't show a European woman naked, but it was okay for an Indian or an African. That's Vikas again. Not that he said as much, but he smirked, and I knew exactly what he was thinking. It's the only time since we got here he's gone back to playing Dr. A, that brilliant young surgeon with opinions on everything.

My favorite part wasn't the circus gallery or the house. It was the statues. There's a "Perseus and Medusa" just outside and even "The Dying Gaul" in a sunken garden full of bougainvillea and hibiscus. The best was the life-sized "David" in front of a row of palm trees. I couldn't take my eyes off those hands. They must be the most beautiful hands in the world, especially the one curled against his right thigh. If I ever met a man with hands like that I don't know what I'd do. Janine would say, "Trust Mrs. A to love hands made of bronze," but a bronze hand can't ignore you, can it? It's always there, never pulling away like yours did that last time. It is the last time, and don't bother trotting out something snide like, "Methinks the lady doth protest too much." No, snide isn't fair, but then you haven't always been fair to me, have you?

Please, please be happy for me. I really am on a second honeymoon, cruises and all.

This afternoon, we left the children with the recreation director and booked ourselves on a yacht called the *Innovation*. Vikas said as soon as we stepped aboard he knew Captain Mike had fought in Vietnam, by the webbing belt wrapped around the compass in front of the wheel. Captain Mike had his wife to help out. They had speakers up on deck and listened to a station that played chestnuts like "Ma Cherie Amour" and "Close to You." Nonstop, so it couldn't have been WLFN RADIO: MORE LOCAL NEWS.

Captain Mike turned out to be the only native Floridian we've met. All the rest are from somewhere else. That's what they call themselves here, sums up their complexions too. Florida may mean land of flowers, but it might just as well have been named for the people, florid from the sun. Vikas says it's unhealthy.

Captain Mike also works as a fishing guide, and he told us things like why people shouldn't fish in shallow water in winter, standing out there in hip waders. It's because in summer the rain dilutes the salt in the intercoastal waterway, and that keeps the sharks out, but in winter the sharks come farther in, so these people are asking for it. We never once left sight of land or an old pink hotel called the Don Cesar, where Captain Mike said F. Scott and Zelda Fitzgerald once stayed. We even went under a drawbridge. The cars make a humming noise when they go over the metal grate, and the faster they go, the higher pitched the hum is from the tires. It was Will, the family musician, who noticed on the first day. He calls them musical bridges.

After an hour's sail, we got into a rubber raft with a motor and got dropped on a barrier island to hunt for shells. It was fairly windy the night before, but we couldn't find many interesting ones. For the children's sake, I gathered a lot of pinkish orange ones called pectin; Vikas found a couple of broken ones called pelican foot. After a while, we realized we were looking in the wrong place. The water's edge is the wrong place to look for shells, because any there are fairly beat up. The best are about thirty feet in, where high tide leaves them to dry in the sun. It's strange walking on sand made of millions of seashells crushed into powder so fine it's like soya flour. I'd nearly given up when I started finding them. Sand dollars.

First one, then another one, then two so tiny they would've made great earrings. I could tell the ones you see in stores are hardened somehow. These were so brittle, if you even waved them in the wind they snapped in two. One of them did, and five V-shaped pieces fell out. They're doves that sing the praises of Christ, like the dove that perched on His shoulder after John baptized Him. That's the woman in the store gushing, not me. Off in the distance rose the pink hotel, and way off, our condo. By the time we turned back, Vikas had a plastic bag filled with pectin and olive and whelk. He'd even found a huge pink Florida roller with its tips broken off. I'd collected a dozen white sand dollars, but I wouldn't put them with the others. I carried them like newborn kittens back to the boat. When we went to climb the short rope ladder, Vikas put them in the zippered pocket of his windbreaker. After we set off, he unzipped his pocket and looked inside.

He hadn't done anything. Hadn't banged against the side of the boat, nothing, but when I reached in the pocket, I pulled out a handful of broken shell as brittle as potato chips. He looked so apologetic, I had to say, "It wasn't your fault," but I kept wishing I'd hung onto them even if it would've made climbing the rope ladder hard. At least I could've taken the blame for them turning back to sand. Then, at the bottom of his pocket, I found five whole ones buried under the chips. I took them out and held them all the way back to the condo. There I took a chance. Don't laugh. I sprayed all five with hair spray. The two I wanted to make earrings from aren't among the five, but that's all right. One day we'll go back, and I'll find more, and I'll know to hang onto them myself. For now I guess I can afford to feel good about things, because I've learned the secret of sand dollars. Know what that is? Once you know where to look, there's no trick to finding your own. The real trick is preserving them.

Speaking of which, we finally got a picture of the five of us together. Till now it's been Vikas with the children, me with the children, the two of us with two of them. They kept saying we should ask somebody to take one with my camera, but I couldn't trust just anyone to get it right. Alma found the answer, made the other two pitch in on a lightweight tripod. Picture me on the beach fussing with the camera, tilting it this way and that, digging the legs first one way, then another into the sand while the children yell, "Hurry, the sun's going down," and Vikas calls, "It doesn't have to be perfect!" Yes it does, and now I've got it on film, safe in my camera, the last picture for the album of this trip.

No, that's Alma showing off her new gold earrings. Hildy's the one in the Mickey Mouse cap. The pink lizard, all orange horns and huge yellow eyes, is Will. That's my Spaceship Earth sweatshirt already needing a wash, and Vikas is finally wearing his. The white dot on the pier? It wasn't supposed to be in the picture but, no, it's not a pelican. He's the man who moved like a gyroscope from the ankles up, flapped his arms and swiveled his wrists and snapped his fingers. The man who loved dancing for the sun.

Ron Block

Abandoned Farmstead

Across the distance of contested lands
behind the shack, the draw ran true to west,
and in the shattered mud and footsteps
turning stone in the sun, the riverbed
cracked and curled into a ruin of shells.
The shack leaned with its walls still parallel.

His father floated in the water trough,
like a space man in his welding mask,
riding a windmill down through clouds of algae,
running molten beads across the cracks so that
triangles in the windmill wouldn't collapse,
worrying as his family drifted off.

He broke the arc to give his eyes a rest
as two dogs passed the house and shrank to dots,
hiding behind the blind spots in his eyes.
The rows of corn converged on the sun, and everything
aside from the sun, which swelled on the horizon,
everything, even distant memories, converged.

He saw the molten sun repair the break
between the days, but when they cooled, they cracked.
Starlight pin-pricks ached inside his eyes.
He dreamed he used his welding wand to fuse
the hinge between a shadow and a tree,
still working at a way to mend his family.

But everything he welded came undone,
the shack collapsing on its own.
Wind whistled through the windmill's skeleton.
The trough went blind with cataracts of moss.
Finally he was lost, drifting into space,
helpless, as his children left the place.

Insolvent, forced to leave himself behind
when sunlight beat the ground to smithereens,
he glanced back through the rear-view mirror,
in a car that shrank upon a shrinking road,
until the last speck of farmstead disappeared.

Messenger

We dance barefoot on fresh-cut straw
as brooms sprout up to sweep us off our feet,
amazed the river's learned to talk,
gargling with a rock stuck in its throat.
Perhaps the waters imitate the winds
that make the trees nod yes yes yes.
We wince and dance and lose our balance.

When Foster asks, "What's wind, one thing or many?"
a hard fall knocks the wind right out of me.
(Crickets tisk behind my back.)
I would say that the wind's an invisible mask,
loosely molded to fit my face
but I've lost my voice. Talking hurts.
I walk the walk of learning how to walk.

Perching in the crotch of its family tree,
a jaybird laughs to mock a crow,
the Heckle and Jeckle of a minstrel show,
does a hawk and sends the other birds rioting,
throws in a cuss word it learned from a cat,
then dives and spears my sandwich wrap,
bobs and swallows, blue scales shining.

While I stumble, trying to catch my breath,
coughing a fit to scare the bird off,
this fool's cap with a cartoon mugger's eyes,
the very malice in a patch of sky,
this mimic doesn't scare, but stares me down,
and coughs back, rasping with its tongue stuck out,
as if hacking were my solitary sound.

A Warning

The jaybird says, "Put on your shoes
or you will know what a broom feels to sweep
and SWEEP and SWEEP-up after you!
Your words all say one thing. 'I'm HERE,' you say.
That's all I get out of you. 'I'm HERE!' As if I CARE?
So what? So what? So what? Sooooo Whaaaaat?

So why don't you listen to me once in a while?
Did you know I can pick seeds from a farmer's beard?
My grandmother was a lizard with blue scales?
You already know that? Well, did you know that
I still have a lizard's tongue? Would you like to see?
Don't you hate these nest-builders, all of them?
Aren't you tired of bullying these silent, timid birds,
cowards all, except my kin, you know them?
The jackdaws, magpies, crows and ravens?

Did you know that I once blinded an owl?
I laughed and laughed. Did you think you could scare me?
You? with your fat naked feet, and—ACK!!
You're ugly and crippled as birds without beaks!
And there's other things you LACK, you LACK!
You LACK, LACK, LACK, LACK, but I lack NOTHING!
So long as I keep my sense of malice!
Because I NEED nothing else, not even my own nest!
And I promise, before the day is through
I'll HAVE your whole sandwich!"

Lunch

The jaybird comes again to hawk for trash
and sweeps in from the woods to stand upon
our picnic table, dancing toward our bread,
puncturing the wrapper with its beak,
and, launching to a nearby limb,
bobs and swallows, unimpressed
by the full range of the human curse
as Foster swings his paddle at the branch,
surprised to see the bird swoop down at him,
making him duck and cover up his head,
heart-pounding and panicked, but surprised to be glad,
glad that he could fight against this bird for food,
glad to curse and have the jaybird cursing back.
This is what he came here for.

Death of the Jaybird

On a broken fishing line,
miscast and twisted around
a cruciform telephone pole
hanging over the Dismal,
we see a jaybird spinning,
hooked through the beak.

Soon its feathers will drop
and its wings will drop
and by pieces the bird will be
carried down the river,
branch to river trunk into the ocean,
the washed-out roots
of a tree growing backwards.

The Power Plant

Along the riverbanks, cottonwoods bloom,
and luminous silk-strands follow the river,
sticking to the green of fireflies.
The dark wind snuffs the candles out
of farmhouses huddled alone in the dark,
and kerosene lamps flicker out to join
the jaybird swelling, blooming from its flesh,
a flickering vapor that rolls ahead of us.

We follow the bloom into a small town,
suspended in a web of power lines.
All lights join the bloom. The porch lights go out.
The neons smeared by rain go blue with cold.
In the cars all the dome lights collapse,
and blue darkness drops on the town like a dim
puppet dropped in a heap of loose string.

We see our halos glowing in the Dismal,
the current teasing our hair.
Our lips are red leaves floating out of our mouths,
floating beneath the bridge, beyond all speaking.
We slip down a tailrace to a water check,
where the boat tips over in the sway and turn.
The bloom slips under, and we're drawn after
into the turbines of the power plant.

Somewhere in a garage, where no shadows move,
and every shadow gathers in one spot,
headlights narrow their pools like a car-struck cat,
as darkness slowly enters through the eyes.

But just as everything seems lost, the moon
lifts its lid a little wider every night,
opens its dead-blue eye in the vivid air
of ozone and thunder where dreams are visible
even when your eyes shut tight.

The dynamo begins to hum again.
Darkness bends away from the light of town.
The power lines snap tight and spark,
and a puppet jerks upright with a glowing face
and prowls down a vein of light reflected in
the Dismal waters as the moon keeps pace,
bursting open on a cottonwood.

"Down in the dump, some tires burnin',
puttin' up a black smudge.
Somebody's fishin' for somethin' he lost,
takes a stick and pokes the rubble,
cursin' his bad luck.

A jaybird's coughin' in the cold, cold evenin'
roughs his feathers, lookin' round
and wonderin' what's he ever gonna do.
A smokin' dump so down and dismal
an owl starts weepin' just to make a sound.

Black flies are boilin', chinless rats are crawlin',
draggin' their full bellies on the ground.
A dead cat flattens as if he's still hidin'
from somethin' that got him
a long time ago.

Now up a black line, there's somethin' or other climbin'
lookin' like two catapillars, breedin' in the sun.
The jaybird dives
and somethin' snags a hold on him,
and flies start to worryin' how to get a bird down.

Down in the dump, somebody's diggin',
lookin' like a mannequin I used to know.
But a new odor's callin' him,
and he ain't even listenin',
he's quiet as a fisherman glued to his pole."

Carol Bly

Male Initiation: An Ancient, Stupid Practice

Any idea bruited about long enough starts to sound true. In the 1960s the stupid idea that sounded true was that *natural* was good, and *civilized* was repressed. Anyone who gives it serious thought realizes that *natural* involves our very worst values:

a) Big things get to eat little things.
b) After procreating the next generation, adults get phased out. That is why you can never interest a periodontist in nature's way. He or she knows that nature's way is that a gum gets sore so you stop flossing and brushing it and then it gets infected and lets loose the tooth it's meant to hold and then you can't eat as well so you get weak and then your brain gets malnourished and then you die. This happens to aging sheep, of course: they are called gummers. People, who often start their intellectual and ethical lives at age fifty, take umbrage at the idea of being phased out at that point.
c) In nature, most of the divergent ideas offered by the occasional innovator are rejected by the group. The more ancient the species the more likely its communities are to divide up into one totalitarian and the thousands of drones. Changing one's ideas to agree with the group ethic is very, very natural.

We are no longer so naive about nature now, but the 1990s have their own psychological naivete and we cling to some false psychological assumptions as wooden-headedly as the French military of 1914 clung to the idea that it was *élan* and morale—not skilled machine-gunnery— which won battles (Barbara Tuchman, in *The Guns of August*). One of the stupidest ideas going about and scarcely challenged is the notion that young males need to "achieve separation from the mother." The modern truth is, they must learn *not* to. There are so many psychologically charming ideas around at any one time, we need some earmarks to judge them by. It is probably wise to suspect any idea which claims to be wafting along on ancient values, joining the wonderful past to the present. It is certainly wise to suspect any movement which says it is against soldiery but in favor of warriorship. Soldiers kill. Warriors kill. What is going on here, psychologically? Someone must be wanting not to stop feeling like a powerful killer—and yet not to look like a violence-lover. What better way than to use an old, romanticized word which will wrap the truth round with Valkyrian shine. It is definitely wise to suspect any psychological fad which says, "You are fine as you ever have been—and as you are. Oh well, you might change your conversation style with your father—but you are and always have been something quite wonderful. It is your heritage!" When that rhetoric comes smoking towards us it's good to be suspicious.

It certainly would be dangerous to believe Carol Gilligan when she insists that women generally are attuned to the feelings and needs of the *other*. A mother cobra comes to mind. A tough white American middle- or upper-class mother comes to mind: a slightly tougher, less white, more newly American, lower-middle-class mother moves into the neighborhood. Then where are all these nurturing feelings which (it is suggested) are the heritage of women? Forget it. The so-called nourishingness of women *inside the community* is one thing: once faced with people who relate to them in business, not love, or in war, not peace, women bring forth the full continuum of hostility just as men have been doing in the same situations.

But it is so hard to drop old assumptions, even when we can see how deplorable they are. The Oliners and other social researchers have shown that people *not* thrown out of the family but raised and kept in love are the most likely to risk their lives to save Jews from Nazis. We know from Alice Miller and others that those treated with cruelty or rejection learn a taste for power plays—the satisfaction of the bully—instead of for friendship (I refer especially to Alice Miller's studies of the young Adolf Hitler).

And in any case, it is hard to drop any idea which works for a powerful contingent of the community. It was very hard for slave-owners to leave off having slaves. It was very hard for British coal-mine operators to stop working children seventeen hours a day "down pit." It is very hard for uneducated males, today, in America, to stop jeering at and often beating their wives: they themselves—with their bad manners and lack of humanities training—tend to be stuck low in our economy: they don't *need* a scapegoat—no one *needs* scapegoats—but it is their taste to have one. Having a scapegoat projects your pain onto the victim, it gives the fun of hurting someone as well—and that is fun for large numbers of males and likely for females to some degree—and it stops painful thinking.

But uneducated males are not the only males suffering from the women's movement. Educated males, too, are being told that the old way was bad and they must change. It is offensive to be told you must change, and we should not be surprised to find a partial male backlash *at every social and educational level.* The psychological backlash is the one that interests us here: why should educated men take to crawling about acting primitive— why should they hanker for the primitive rite of dis-civilizing the young male? What would be the attraction of dis-civilizing anyone?

We need to make guesses about what those males are thinking. I say "those males" because there are tens of thousands of men who rejoice in the women's movement toward justice just as Oliver Wendell Holmes rejoiced in his dissenting opinions to make justice where there had not been justice before. Justice is a complex taste: once you have it you never give it up. In this essay, however, I want to think about males for whom dreamy habit is lots dearer than the idea of new justice for women. Here is what I am guessing they think or half-consciously feel:

1. It used to be all right to exercise the rights of "the male ego": now they are taking it away from us!
2. I had the male ego and it meant I didn't feel the kind of pain which makes people protect underdogs. (For example, who doesn't know a beautiful junior-high-school girl who lets herself act like a living room bully all her life because she always was just fine as is? —she didn't *have* to be nice: only the weak must be nice. Everyone knows that.)
3. The past—the roistering about, the noncommunication with any dull women around the house—it was so nice! Can't we stick with that?
4. I think I will distract attention from women-as-victims by making up "male issues"—I will get the conversation to go back to all-about-men! If people will just stop looking at the victims' psychological bruises—how shall I do that?—Ah, *I* will have psychological bruises! I will have some, too! Then people will all look at me again.

Those are my guesses about whims and parts of thoughts, tags of anger and disappointed ego, which may be lurching and buffeting about inside the heads of some thousands of educated men.

I would like to move on to explain what happens, psychologically, when you separate for any reason the young males of any species from hearth and home. If we look at what the psychological habitat and nourishment of the male is *within the household* and what it is when he is forced out—by convention or by initiation rites—we can decide on whether "achieving separation from the mother" is good or bad or a mixed bag.

In farm tomcats: if you chase the young male off the farm, it will die or join a band of wild, roving tomcats, who systematically visit farmsteads where kittens have just been born. The kittens' mother will fight ferociously, but often the tomcats succeed in biting each kitten's neck so it dies. I have seen it again and again. If the male cat, on the other hand, is encouraged to stay around the yard and be a home-based mouser like the mother, it sometimes turns out protective of kittens.

In primitive tribes of people, the grown males do little work and a good deal of slamming around painting up for dancing and killing. Young boys respect their mothers and sisters and homes until one day or one night they are torn away by their aging-recess-playground fathers. The old males usually do some slight physical damage to the boys, and they invariably terrify them. (It is important to note that *all* initiation rites involve psychological abuse of some kind: something you once loved gets insulted. Something you once were gets told to change.) The young primitive boy can never "go backward"—the rite says—to the mother—to the circle of love: therefore, he must, psychologically speaking, eat crow: he must humiliate himself by loving those who have tortured him. He has been dis-cultivated.

Dis-cultivation is what a Drill Instructor must do. It is interesting that he does not do it of necessity. A young man who studies what it would be to be a good Marine does not get past the Drill Instructor's humiliations: he, too, has to go through having his personal truths *undone* and made regressive. He is forced to lie. He must shout, in unison with others, MURDER IS FUN! MURDER IS FUN! (Please see P.J. Caputo's great book, *A Rumor of War*.) The point of the initiation is to learn that what you *were* is nothing—or at least, less.

Then here is the next psychological step: once someone is convinced that he is nothing, or at least, less, you give him a psychological tidbit to feed on. You have taken away trust in individuality, his trust in his own thinking and ethics—but in return, you give him a sub-ethical treat: he is allowed and encouraged actually to believe that his close-in group, his squad—not even his platoon yet—just his squad—is the best. The others are less. Your squad is good. You yourself have no value, but the squad has.

Now that is very uncomplex, unnourishing psychological food, but it serves the uses of a violent culture and it says, as well, to the squad-member: "You do not need to become, not ever, a complex person who will ever have to stand alone. The ideas we give you (such as anything *other* is wrong—it is all right to hurt them [the enemies of the United States]) are not civilized ideas but at least you can have them *in your group*, all together, and that's comforting, isn't it? Being together in a group?" Drill Instructors never talk about lemmings.

People trained in the humanities sometimes, but not always, resist such dis-civilization. Therefore, the Volkspolizei of the former East Germany, when recruiting people for special (torturing) squad work, chose farm boys from Saxony. They didn't need to choose sadists; they just needed people not in the psychological habit of talking about the pull we all feel to bully, the pull we all feel to cling to outmoded comforts, and so on. These boys had not had conversations about the greatest of all twentieth-century ethics: that the idea is to widen and widen the circle of what one feels tolerant of until it includes even other species. It is much easier to make and keep a vicious-pack person if that person has not heard the respectful conversations of educated, humane homes.

People rather like complex ethical problems if they get to bandy them back and forth in conversation. They tend to learn the arts of tolerance and of talk.

The last part of our century is the era of tolerance and talk. The old male style—noncommunication with women, indeed with anyone who is *other*—is now out of fashion. That is threatening, apparently, not just to the hard drinker at the Legion, but to some educated males. C.G. Jung's whole theory of the *animus* in women is an elaborate way of putting down women— as if they had some crippling psychology which he must make much rhetoric of.

No matter how long-standing the notion is, male separation rites do evil. They support the old, bad, natural male regression; they divide those with power to hurt from those with the quiet habits of love. It is a process which pains modern, unthreatened men as much as it delights male revisionists.

But I would like to describe an odd, bad side-effect which male separation brings about: it deprives young women of fire just as surely as it deprives the young male of complex tolerance and affection. We all know how dull it is to talk to those women (now in their fifties and sixties and seventies and eighties) who are suppressed by males: their conversation is all *enabling* and *sticky-supportive* and generally concept-free. So many of them are angry, too—yet still unconscious of the anger—that wrath seeps into much that they say. I won't go into that more because it has been studied and reported a lot. No one expects prisoners or fiefs to make humorous, serious, connection-filled conversations. Of course such women are dull. Psychologists report that they have been jeered at two and a half times as much, and interrupted two times as much, as men in their age groups.

Alas, male separation endangers the intellectual sport of young women as well. They slide into bland, polysyllabic language instead of saying what they feel with brevity and verve. It is so difficult to preserve sharp language in our culture. Women are much pressed to use words like "concerns" instead of "wrath" or "grief." "Concerns!" It is a horrible word! But it is hard for young women to say, "I was infuriated with . . ." They are still pressed to say, instead, "I have a problem with . . ."

At first I thought it was *only* women who used such flaccid, evasive self-expression. Then I began reading things by men in the men's movement. I found more of it. So we need to keep males and females together—not separate them—if only to save some clarity in their talk! Clarity and speed are hard for human beings, in any case: nature (not elegant civilization) thrives on skillfully organized, thoroughly mediocre minds willing to give up individual ethic in order to support some *ad hoc* group project! That's nature! Bees! And that's corporate life! It is also domestic life—whenever we allow it to be that way.

I add that point about women's language in order to show that women had better not spend all their time in packs, either. They will lose surprise and complexity. And when surprise and complexity of *language* go, enough ethical boredom sets in to drive anyone into wrathfully leaving. I have read a number of books by men who have joined the army or the Marine Corps and then regretted it. Some of them were men who had *read* Erich Maria Remarque: they shouldn't have been as surprised as they were to find out how real war is. I have finally guessed that it must be that American life is so unethical, so morally boring, and the language around our houses is so bland and without idea or risk, that anyone with verve clambers out of the home—even if it means backward into a brutal direction.

If we vastly underestimate how much fun it has been for men to bully their sons through initiations and to bully their wives through insult, I think we also vastly underestimate how bored we shall all be if we don't encourage one another to use complex, fast-moving language and to take on the complex, furious projects of real civilization.

Just eschewing the drivel about ancient rites alone is going to take some passionate male, and female, work.

Di Brandt

completely seduced
by motherhood,

this is how you got
through the day

without sleep,
without pay,

without help,
words,

companions,
a break.

your mind bouncing
off walls,

& the ceiling
& the floor,

eyes blurred
with exhaustion.

you weren't thinking
about that.

you weren't thinking
about your stretched

skin.

you saw yourself
in the dark pool

of your baby's eyes,
shining,

a goddess, the source,
the very planet.

your breaths flowing
together,

your breasts filled
with milk & honey.

all night, you were
the earth,

rocking.

(later you shrank
into an ordinary

middle-aged woman,
enjoying sleep.

amused by the ordinary
world,

half mother,
half not mother.

bewildered by time
and place,

& wrinkled skin.
& missing children.)

the day my sister left us
i cried into the night,

for the family script
which kept us bound

together around the table,
the wedding feast,

for eternity, we thought.

i cried for my father
who tried so hard to be God,

to make the world permanent
for us, & died that way,

not knowing the first human
thing about us.

i cried for the words which
kept us there,

around the table, gagged
& bound,

with blood on our hands,
but sanctified, & holy.

our suffering made
the story true.

i cried because my sister
went away,

so i could come back.

because she knew herself
as the outsider,

the third daughter, the after-
thought,

& i am not.

for twenty years i've been
running away

from the family, & the Bible
& God.

i cannot reach across
my own abandonment.

i cannot cry for my mother,

who won't forgive me
for refusing her comfort,

insisting on my separate,
inconsolable pain.

i ache tonight with being
alone.

i ache, former baby sister,
because you are gone.

you have marked the outer
edge of the family cliff

& will jump it, & i will stay
behind.

you have left me, baby sister
as i once left you,

motherless, grieving.

your absence translates
into my return:

to the empty table,
the spilled wine,

the holes where our faces
might have been,

the family gibberish.

trees are not enough.
the way the light

falls on the snow,
blue, & gold,

the long shadows,
the cold diamond

sparkle of it.

i'm looking hard
at all of this,

the bare branches
feathering the sky,

pale orange, lemon.

i'm trying hard
not to feel the rage

burning in my head,
arms, chest, all of me,

flaming, this sullen
winter afternoon.

some days i just can't
bear it,

the world's weight
on me, & i

a woman, alone,
carrying it.

poems are lovely
too, a consolation,

holding me, as much
as anything,

to what is human.
but words are also

not enough.
the roomful of

informed citizens
discussing their

urbane humanity
is not enough.

(you were not enough.)

the air is big & open
& will hold

all my screaming,
i think.

it's hard to be held
in air,

the arms of the goddess
brushing you lightly

as you float by.

last night i became
an Iraqi woman,

wailing over
her lost sons,

*Wafiq, Amin,
my firstborn,*

*my beloved
babies,*

*shot down like dogs
in the desert.*

the night before
i was a prisoner

lining up for food,
a pill pressed

into my forehead
like a diamond,

birth control,
they said,

so i could be raped
without getting

pregnant,
prison rules.

this morning
i'm Canadian,

safe, well fed,
& civilized:

not believing
in poetry

only in bombs.

give us this day
our daily bomb.

that's what keeps us
happy, isn't it,

keeps us safe
at night?

when you wake up
shaking, isn't that

what you think,
Reader? how lucky

you are to be living
on the most heavily

defended continent
on the face of earth,

how lucky we are
to have so many

BOMBS

for Ali, age 11

that day, when i became
a lost baby again,

& you the big sister,
we walked through the Bay.

& you showed me the flowers,
& the soaps, & the perfume.

& you stopped me from buying
everything.

& we remembered together
where the door was,

& how to get home.
& you called my baby rage

King Kong. & you made up
a little song, for me,

finding our way to the pound,
to pick up our lost dog.

is this Logan?
is this Logan?
is this Logan?
is this Logan?

& when we found it we chanted,
LO GAN LO GAN LO GAN LO GAN

oh, you were so wise that day,
big sister, little daughter,

& i, i was so loved.

Bonnie Burnard

Figurines

The figurines, a prepubescent boy and girl, are a foot high, and hollow. The boy is dressed in a creamy sailor top, blue britches and a wide-brimmed hat. He stands holding an upright oar, his left arm hugging it close to his body, his eyes fixed on some puzzling middle distance. His strawberry blond hair is very long and thick. The girl, plump by today's standards and fairly self-assured by the set of her jaw, wears a summer frock with a dropped waist, a voluptuous satin sash encircling her hips; in the crook of her elbow she holds, too tightly, a half-crushed nosegay. Her hair, the color of pale beach sand, is longer still and thicker, falling heavily on her shoulders. I imagine these children to be cousins, on an outing near a lake.

The clay, painted by a steady hand in summer white and soft pastels, blue and pink and apple green, and a fleshy peach, could be from anywhere. The figurines are not attributed to anyone or to any time; there are no markings on the bases. This disappoints me, more than seems reasonable.

I've stood them on a high glass shelf in my curio, just under the lights. There is a good chance my dinner guests see them as coy artifacts from some impossible past and, of course, they are.

The figurines were a gift to my great-aunt Lottie when she was a young, unmarried nurse. This would have been in the early twenties, the reputedly roaring twenties when there were women in her world who happily grabbed the opportunity after a God-awful war to be frivolous, who drank bathtub gin and wore dresses with layered fringe that swung out from their bodies and snapped back again as they danced. She lived in with a family while the aged father died, tending to him. She told me this. He must have needed whatever it was only a nurse could administer to ease him through it, something from a chemist, something respected and dangerous in the wrong hands. Whatever his need, I imagine her fulfilling it with the same detached care she used in very late middle age, when I knew her. When the work was completed, the figurines were given to her, either in payment or above payment, in gratitude. On her death they were given to my mother and came through her to me.

The figurines do not give off any particular sense of my aunt. You would not imagine any connection between her and these elegant clay children unless you saw them, as I did, sitting on a gate-legged oak table in her living room, just behind a cut glass humbug dish. They had been a gift and she'd taken them and incorporated them into her life; that's what people like her did with gifts. She would not have thought to ask if she could perhaps exchange them for something a little more to her liking. It's possible that they had not been purchased for her at all but were esteemed family possessions. It's possible that they had been a gift another time, valued and held in good keeping, and then given again.

I have no idea what she saw when she looked at the figurines. Perhaps her patient had died independently, taking care to keep the biggest part of the task for himself, resisting the need to make demands when no one with a good heart could refuse him. Perhaps there were children who brought her tea after her nap and asked if they could touch her hair. It's equally possible that she disliked the family. The room they'd assigned to her might have been cold, the blankets rough, the children precociously rude. Though I could be angry if I believed she was badly treated, she gave no hint one way or the other.

We saw Aunt Lottie once a week, every week, every year, when we picked her up for church and delivered her gratefully home again, and she was there with us for Christmas, just off to the side in her chair by the buffet, smiling quickly at children, running her fingers whenever she could through a thick head of hair, and largely ignoring the kitchen work. She behaved like a guest, behavior I have always admired.

Often on Sunday mornings I was sent from the car to her front door to tell her we'd arrived and sometimes I would be placed in her living room while she searched for mislaid summer gloves or a book she'd promised one of her friends at church, history usually. I was always invited to help myself to a humbug and I always did, replacing the cut glass lid gingerly, aware of noise and the possibility of shattered glass. On the wall above the figurines the Serenity Prayer was offered in a framed petitpoint sampler: 'God give us grace to accept with serenity the things that cannot be changed, courage to change the things which should be changed, and the wisdom to distinguish the one from the other.' God was entirely in upper case letters, as were grace and serenity and courage and wisdom, as if the woman who had worked the needle wanted to ensure no misunderstanding, as if she'd plowed these elegant, aristocratic words across a wheat field, intending them to be visible from a great distance. Sitting beside the figurines, sucking on a humbug, I generously granted an appropriateness to the prayer, because my aunt was old, because she had been weakened.

She had been widowed early and I don't know how she lived or who took care of her financially, though someone must have. There were no pension plans available to her, no big insurance policies on the lives of men who might die young. Her husband John had had a farm, there, in Ontario, which he'd sold off when they made their move to the west, sometime in the late twenties. There had been a son, Billy, and I think I remember pictures of Billy, at five or six, wearing short wool pants and good dark shoes, bright-looking, with the prairie behind him as a backdrop. But maybe I've never seen his picture. Perhaps I've confused him with other boys in short wool pants and good shoes who were placed against a backdrop of crops for their pictures. He drowned in the West, in a slough, although I know nothing about the circumstances. I don't know if he was wild and headstrong, forever beyond the reach of his mother's protective hands, or dreamy and clumsy, given to wandering off and forgetting to come back for his midday meal. I do know they returned to Ontario within a year of his drowning.

I was gone by the time she was elderly. I went home only

occasionally and during one of these visits my father obliquely insisted that I accompany him to the seniors' home where she lived. I don't know who moved her there, or how it played out. My father, her nephew, is a man of habits and regularity; he saw her every Sunday, as he had through all the other years. She was well into her seventies and her mind was wild with Alzheimer's, though her body stayed fairly sound. I was twenty-two, full of myself and stupid enough to think she might be interested in my travels. As we walked up the sidewalk toward the home's wide doors, my father advised me just to smile and not to take her up on anything she might say.

I doubt if I could have found her on my own, though they had her properly dressed, her two rings still on her fingers, her lips a pale, respectable pink. She was sitting in a wheelchair, tied upright with soft thick bands of bleached white cloth, though that's only the visitor talking, they would not have been soft from her perspective. She didn't know me, I was not in the world her mind recognized. Only once or twice did she call my father by his own name.

She was beyond self-discipline and rude, to my father, to the other patients, to the nurses and doctors who stopped to touch her shoulder and speak to us. She used language which I imagined to be new to her, mumbling saucy remarks in response to any attention she received. She was boastful. She talked of running a hospital single-handedly, surrounded by idiots who would not take their responsibilities seriously. She spoke with hatred about the prairie, so big you couldn't find anything, couldn't be heard above the filthy wind. "Damn the prairie," she said, squinting, looking to me for complicity.

My father had said we would stay an hour and we did. We drank the coffee offered by a volunteer, a woman I didn't know, and we each took a generous piece of fruit bread from a silver tray. My sister-in-law was at the home working as a volunteer, busy elsewhere, but she came over once and stood behind the wheelchair, wrapped her arms around my aunt's shoulders and kissed her hair. This gesture prompted a shy grin to break across the small, closed face.

When the hour was over and we were in the car I asked my father had she really run a hospital somewhere and he said yes, a small one, they were all small then, and many of them were run by women not unlike her. He said she'd been a strong and capable and responsible young woman, words which I took as comment on my own activities as well as context for the small obscenities she'd used. I laughed and said good for her. I repeated one of the milder phrases she'd used with such panache. I said, "Maybe she's been a lady too long." I said, "Good for you, Aunt Lottie." My father tried to laugh, reluctant to push me farther away than I'd already gone, but then he turned his face from me, as he had not once turned from my aunt. "No," he said. "It has not been good for her. It has rarely been good for her."

After the drowning, when she returned with her husband to Ontario, my knowledge of her story runs thin. My father told me that day in the car that he'd always had a good deal of respect for John, for his determination to go out west and break new ground. He said there wasn't land enough for third sons at home, that what looked like choice wasn't always choice. He said when they came back to Ontario they came pretty much empty-handed and that arrangements had to be made to get them resettled. So John did farm again, on somebody's land. He lived for a while after they went back, before she became middle-aged and then old, searching for summer gloves while the church bells rang all over town and I sat in a straight-backed chair eating her humbugs, glancing occasionally at the Serenity Prayer, touching, more than once, her figurines.

She brought the figurines west, she packed them and brought them with her on the train; the idea was to leave for good, to make a new home. And she took them back to Ontario with her when it was over, though there is no evidence of movement, I can't find even the smallest chip.

I did not go back to Ontario for my aunt's funeral; it's not practical to make the trip for every death. She was rarely in my thoughts. We had our children. Their needs and the necessities which bounced off the walls of this house kept me, as they say, busy.

And then my mother died. I returned and stayed for a while, claiming my share of the grief, taking my part of the work made necessary by death. As is the custom, people gathered at the house, coming in without knocking, carrying practical casseroles wrapped in newspaper and still-warm baking, leaving sometimes in the middle of a sentence when a chair was needed. Someone, a young neighbor I didn't know, raked the lawn. There was talk, in contrived, ordinary language, of the distribution of my mother's belongings, which my father allowed and encouraged; nearly everyone connected to her valued something. I refused to take part in these discussions. I sat in all the rooms, I walked from room to room, I picked up the things she had accumulated and put them down again where she had placed them. When I saw the figurines in her living room, I saw nothing.

Not very long after my mother's death, my father shipped her feathery crystal dinner bell west to me, securely packed with the other things she had apparently named mine, some silver, a Royal Doulton grandmother, a pickle cruet, a magnificent lace tablecloth which I had fingered nervously as a child sitting at the dinner table. At the bottom of the box, because of their weight, were the figurines. He'd enclosed a note, listing the contents and telling me I had asked for the figurines the last time I saw my aunt, did I remember? I didn't remember asking. I wondered if he might have imagined it, or if he had simply decided that something which should have been true, was true.

As my aunt's executor, he had arranged that these clay children come like a gift to our family, first to my mother, and eventually to me. Because he wanted me not just to have them, but to want them. I repacked the box from Ontario, carried it upstairs and pushed it to the back of the spare room closet.

I have accumulated more than enough on my own over the years, selecting things carefully, placing them deliberately around us, my taste becoming more and more selective, more and more trustworthy. Uncomfortable with disarray and pleased with my pragmatism, I long ago sold the wedding gifts that did not suit me at a neighborhood garage sale, remembering the giver briefly as I washed and priced each item.

But my father, who with his habits and regularity and his packing of boxes has become death's familiar, has been joined in his campaign by my son, who is oblivious but no less insistent.

This summer at Waskesiu, halfway up the hill with my binoculars in search of his father and sisters, who were fishing on the lake, their silhouette indistinguishable against the multicolored pastel prairie sunset, I turned and found my lanky sunburned son standing on the beach, hugging one of the paddles from his inflatable raft. His arms and legs were caked with sand, his face dazed with exhaustion and accomplishment. Not a very complex or unique vision. I'd seen him before in a similar pose.

Perhaps it was only the distance between us, between his position on the sand at the edge of the water and mine on the hill under the poplars.

They have conspired against me, closed in around my middle age, their lives brushing mine if I move. I am not exactly unhappy about this. I have adjusted.

My curio, bought with the money we had long protected from overdue income tax and a paint job for the roof, is honey-colored oak, with a light, and leaded panes. It's quite big, too big for the dining room, but it holds a lot. The slightly tarnished silver is on display, and the Royal Doulton grandmother, and the pickle cruet, and the bell. The figurines sit on their own glass shelf just under the light, turned one toward the other; pale children stranded in innocence.

I have begun to ask certain people if they will leave me things, specific things, chosen by me and identified as mine in their wills. I am not nearly brave enough to depend on chance. My aged father's lawyer can worry about his Bell Canada shares and whatever else there is; I have no doubt it will be fairly distributed according to my father's directions, which are none of my business. I want his battered *Testament*, the guidelines of his time and place, which is in fact a dialogue, the margins full of doubts and opinions and possibilities. I expect to find evolution in these doubts and opinions and possibilities, which I will be able to track by the diminishing strength of his hand. I expect to find hope and heartache and stamina. I expect to find clues. When I asked for the *Testament* during a Sunday phone call, he made me listen for a minute to dead air. He said he'd see; he said I wasn't the only one interested.

I have wondered, of course, what I have to leave, and who might want what. I've looked around. Who, for instance, among everyone I've ever known, will want my mother's silver, my jade rings, my books, the coy figurines?

Sharon Butala

Absences

Although I never notice them anymore, when I was a child I *saw* elevators. They seemed beautiful and mysterious to me, the Notre Dame Cathedral, the Edinburgh Castle of our prairie villages, and as inevitable, as right, as were the fields of grain around them. I never questioned where they had come from and, more to the point, what they were for, though, looking back, I doubt I knew, since my father wasn't a farmer.

But I do remember how, every fall on our way to school, when we reached the railroad tracks, we would be excited to find a long line of trucks parked for a good block, each loaded with wheat, each with its single driver, snaking its way into the elevator. I even remember playing Twenty Questions at school on one of those endless, itchy Friday afternoons in spring and choosing for my subject "The Prairie Sentinel" (I must have read it somewhere), which nobody could guess, and when I told them, made nobody any the wiser, though the elevator was as ubiquitous a presence in our lives as toast for breakfast or the vegetable garden out behind the house. And I must have assumed that, like all things of the adult world, elevators had always been there and always would be.

I didn't know it, but the golden age of wooden elevators had already peaked before I was born, in 1938, when there were over 5000 of them dotting the prairie. The first ones were set nine to ten miles apart because a farmer hauling with a team and wagon could make only about twenty miles or one round trip in a day. A lot of factors contributed to the decline of the wooden elevator, but probably the depression, which caused radical changes in all aspects of prairie life, was the most significant. Many farms were abandoned, rural population declined, remaining farms got bigger so there wasn't need for elevators to be so close together. Besides that, roads began to improve and farmers to haul grain in trucks, making it easier to go further. At the same time, the multitude of small grain companies began to amalgamate. Many of the old wooden elevators were too small to be profitable—traffic of about a half million bushels annually is considered to be the break-even point by grain companies and 30,000 bushels per track mile by the railways—and with each amalgamation more elevators were torn down. The railways too began to abandon unprofitable lines and elevators on those lines fell into disuse. By 1985 there were fewer than 2000 working elevators left on the prairies. The number continues to decline.

In their place the new wooden elevators hold about 160,000 bushels—two full plastic grocery bags hold about a bushel—and the latest technology builds them of concrete with a capacity of around 330,000 bushels. (There are a few inland terminals too, which can hold more than a half million bushels.) These all dwarf the small wooden elevators which sometimes still stand trackside next to them with an air of pathetic bravery, and they change drastically the prairie skyline. Instead of the sloping roof of the traditional elevator, their roofs are flat and have a series of distributor pipes mounted on them which direct the grain to the different bins. And they have contraptions attached to the sides for elevating the grain, for cleaning it and for cleaning the air inside. Nor are the concrete structures as colorful. The wooden ones were painted a deep wine or a brilliant orange with gold roofs—Pioneer Grain still paints its elevators these colors—but the concrete ones are, well, the color of concrete, and all of them look like what they are: the no-nonsense, technologically up-to-date workplace of a huge commercial enterprise.

For more than eighty years the wooden elevator has been the most telling symbol of the Canadian prairies, partly because it is our only truly indigenous architecture (since the demise of the sod hut), and because on the vast, empty plain it was the first sign to herald the welcome presence of people. And its very simplicity of design suited the stark sweep of land and enormous sky and was always visually exciting, a stimulating subject for artists.

There used to be a town on the Trans-Canada highway near Swift Current called Antelope. It was already a ghost town when I first saw it and I barely noticed it when I passed except as a landmark that brought me closer to my destination. Before long the few remaining buildings had vanished. I noted this and forgot it. Then one day I drove by to find the elevators had been torn down and the lumber hauled away, leaving nothing to mark where Antelope had been.

Coming upon the place so suddenly, I hadn't time to prepare myself, and the emptiness at that windswept grassy spot struck a deep chord of loss in me. All the bereavements prairie people have had to endure these last few years—closures of businesses, post offices and schools, losses of land and neighbors—swept over me and I slowed, seeing those phantom elevators in my mind's eye. Now I never go by there without remembering them, and I never fail to mourn their passing. Their absence has become as poignant and powerful as their presence used to be, marking as it does the demise of the last symbol of the world my generation of Great Plains dwellers knew.

Things Fall Apart

It was always like this: the alarm rang, Jack shut it off, he turned to Rosemary, she slept on, yet as soon as he touched her, she was awake. It occurred to him to wonder if she only pretended to be asleep, if she lay there morning after morning, year after year, waiting for his touch before she could begin her day. This thought warmed, then aroused him and he pushed closer to her, nuzzling her cheek, her ear, her hair, while she smiled with her eyes still closed.

The radio went on in Susan's room. Rock music at seven in the morning. Though her school was only two blocks away, Susan had taken to rising earlier and earlier in order to give herself time for a long shower and another half-hour to perfect her makeup and hair and to put together the right outfit. At fourteen, she was as expert with cosmetics as a professional model. Jack and Rosemary found this both appalling and funny. But her radio was so loud it almost drowned out theirs and Rosemary sat up, the moment between the two of them lost.

And now Mark and small Jilly were out of bed, one closing the bathroom door, the other padding down the hall into their bedroom.

"Hi, Jilly Bean," Rosemary said. She was out of bed now, picking Jill up in her arms, carrying her from the room, trailing the dressing gown she hadn't had time to finish putting on.

"Turn that radio down, Susie," Jack called, knowing she couldn't hear him. He'd have to do it himself.

The smell of coffee had already drifted upstairs, thanks to a timer on the electric coffee percolator. The morning sun shone through the window in the front door at the bottom of the stairs and lit the hallway with a clean, pure light. Mark came out of the bathroom; Jack rested his hand for a second on top of Mark's small round head and felt his still-silky, fine hair under his fingers and palms. He stopped at the door to Susan's room.

Abruptly the noise of the radio diminished and this too, it occurred to him, happened every morning. He heard Jilly's small voice chirping away in the kitchen and Rosemary murmuring her answer, he heard Mark humming softly to himself in the next room, and he heard Susan drop something to the floor and the rustling as she bent to pick it up. All the sounds, all the smells of his family surrounded him, moved deep inside him; he felt how the very molecules of his being were intermingled with theirs, and theirs with his. In an instant it seemed to him that he and his family had together woven a tapestry that was patterned and richly textured with the contents of each life, yet their mutual love gave it order. He tested it and found it strong; more than serviceable, it was also beautiful. He wept, standing outside his teenage daughter's room in the sunny fall morning, at the sheer goodness of life. He wept silently and nobody heard him.

At ten o'clock he walked into his first meeting of the day. Although his work took him into the city's schools daily, he never went into one without first having to overcome reluctance, even a slight sense of dread. He was not sure where this had come from; his own school experience had not been especially unpleasant, nor did Susan's and Mark's appear to be. Yet, if the truth were told, despite his Master's degree in Education, he despised schools, loathed them, and could not convince himself that they did anything in the long run but harm. This feeling he kept secret from everyone. He kept thinking that one day he would hit upon a system for educating the children of the nation that would not be so difficult for them or so frequently stupidly painful. In the meantime, here he was, working in schools every day as if he believed in their necessity, their efficacy.

Kent, the principal, was waiting for him.

"The others are in the staff lounge," he said. "It's the only place we have to meet till the renovations are finished." Jack had come to see about a twelve-year-old named Todd McKenzie. The boy no longer paid attention in class and his homework was never done; always a quiet child, he had become so silent that his teachers feared for his mental health. He had taken to doing some pretty strange things, too.

"Strange? Like what?" Jack asked. The boy's classroom teacher was present, Mr. Woloshyn, a trim, handsome man who would be principal himself in another year or two if Jack didn't miss his guess. He knew the type from long experience. Also present was Frank Sutherland, the gym teacher, a lazy, uncomplicated man who was trying to get through to his retirement with as little effort or trouble as possible. And a young woman he hadn't met before named Jade. Privately, he thought it a ridiculous name, although she was striking despite a too-big nose and thick, long hair that needed a good brushing. She was the school's newly acquired art specialist: "Art, drama, but no music," she said. "We have an Itinerant for that."

Mr. Woloshyn said, "He hangs around after school when all the other kids are long gone and wants to clean the boards for me. He wants to hand out notebooks or run errands—he's driving me crazy with his over-eagerness. To be perfectly honest," he said, crossing one leg over the other and smoothing his pant-leg with one well-tended hand, "I'm concerned about his sexual orientation." He glanced around the group quickly, surreptitiously, assessing the reaction to this. He was trying to be up-to-date and fearless, Jack knew, wanting to impress the Consultant; these things had a way of filtering back to the Superintendent's office.

"Does he touch you?" Jack asked, to discomfit him.

Mr. Woloshyn colored and said, "No, but he stands too close to me, that's what I find worrisome. It's too close."

Jack nodded.

"His relationship with the other kids is becoming more and more troubled," Kent, the principal, said. "I've had him in my office three times in the last week."

"What happens?" Jack asked.

"He wanders by himself almost like an autistic kid. When somebody approaches him, he turns on them, fights them."

Jade, the art teacher, moved impatiently. "I think he's hungry," she said. "He's thin as a rail."

"Can't do a damn thing in gym class," Frank said. "Doesn't even try. I got so disgusted with him the other day I put him on the bench and let him stay there through the whole period."

"How did he take that?" Jack asked.

Frank shrugged. "He didn't say anything. Sat and looked at his shoes for an hour."

"Have you talked with his parents?"

"Ahh, his parents," Kent said.

"His mother works, his father's gone," Mr. Woloshyn said. "I asked her to come in twice now. Both times she hasn't shown."

"That's why we called you in, Jack," Kent said. "Can you find out what's going on?"

When the meeting was over Mr. Woloshyn shook Jack's hand briskly, then left. The gym teacher had wandered away some time before. Kent said, "Can you find your own way out? I've got a meeting five minutes ago." He bounded away up the stairs. Jade came and stood behind him, touched his arm. He turned to her.

"Come to the art room," she said softly. "I've got something to show you." They walked side by side, their heels clicking on the polished tile floor. She was almost as tall as Jack, and he thought fondly of small, plump Rosemary. Jade had set up a display of paintings on easels in the empty, sunny room. They were done with tempera on big sheets of newsprint tacked to boards. He glanced at them, looked inquiringly at Jade, but she said nothing, meeting his eyes with a steady gaze.

"He did them all since the beginning of the school year?"

She nodded. "I told him he could come anytime he wants to. He comes every day, when there aren't any other kids here."

Each painting began carefully as a house, a few people, a bird, a tree, a sun. Each one was stroked over with a whirling mass of black or purple, the clean, orderly beginning exploded each time into tumult.

"Good for you," he said to Jade. Tears were rushing to his eyes again, and he remembered the moment earlier that morning in the hallway of his house.

"It's nothing," she said. He could feel her anger. "He has no home, he has no father, he's unhappy," she said. "And either he's not getting enough to eat or he's anorexic. It's no big deal." Their gazes met again, her large dark eyes holding his.

"It's no good," he said finally. "You'll see so many of these kids, you'll have to stop caring or it'll kill you."

She flushed, looked away. "I saw you," she said. "Don't give me useless advice you can't even listen to yourself." He was stunned by her directness, her force.

"What'll we do?" he asked her after a moment. He saw she understood that he meant about all the Todd McKenzies in their world and the way he and Jade felt about them.

"It was ever thus?" she asked him. He saw that her fingernails were chewed to the quick, her hands thick-veined and strong, the skin rough. Despite all the housework Rosemary did, her small hands were silky smooth, her fingernails always shaped with an emery board and shiny with polish. And she smelled so sweet, like a child, his Rosemary.

"I think—" he said, "—I decided after I'd been doing this work for a few years and realized that I hadn't seen one iota of progress or even real change, that if I could make one kid's day a little easier, just one day, it'd be worth doing." He gestured, then shrugged. They studied each other, standing in the sunshine in front of Todd McKenzie's paintings.

"Once you know this," she said slowly, "it seems there's no place you can go to forget it."

He thought gratefully of his home, his children. "You have to try very hard," he said.

She stood motionless, turned slightly away from him, staring into space. "I do have my art," she said. "I'm a sculptor." She lifted her hands toward him, palms up. She smiled and abruptly he wanted to kiss her. "I can forget everything then." She seemed to be speaking to herself. He turned vaguely away from her, troubled, went to the window, touched one of Todd's pictures. It felt stiff and cold under his fingertips.

The center cannot hold, he thought. He dropped his hand, looked back at her, found her watching him with an expression that held nothing back.

"We could run away together to a deserted tropical isle," she said. Her voice was husky. "Leave this behind." She had stopped smiling.

In the late afternoon he had to go to a school in a new suburb on the farthest side of the city from his home. Afterward, driving home on the highway that circled the city's outer edge, as he always did, he tried to put the day out of his mind. It was early evening, rush hour was over and there were few cars on this long stretch of road. The sky had clouded over, a light rain had begun to fall and the air had grown chilly.

He turned the heater on low and the wipers onto intermittent. The radio played softly, barely audible over the steady hum of the motor. He found himself tired, not far from something he held back all the time and feared was despair. He drove on, not thinking.

He saw Jade's face, those large, pain-filled dark eyes, and heard her voice, husky, yet strong. That she was not beautiful pleased him. She had a magnetism that held him, even now, even though if he chose not to, he would never have to see her again.

But no. It had happened.

As he drove homeward alone through the dusk, the future unfolded before him with a dull but perfect clarity. He would phone her, they would have lunch together. Another time, before long, he would go to her apartment, they would make love. They would fit together like hand and glove, already they understood each other, and that understanding would grow till they were one person, one soul.

He would leave Rosemary and his children. All this he could see: that in time he would even be able to detach himself from Rosemary's suffering. He could see it would last two years, before she would begin to heal. He would offer her support, he would be patient with her sorrow, her rage, her suicide attempt. He would do whatever he could for her and for his beloved children, but he would spend all the foreseeable future and more with Jade. She was his destiny, and he hers.

A car behind him honked and he jumped, found himself at the lights where he turned off the highway onto the main street of his suburb. He stepped on the gas, turned, and turned again, wondering that his daydream had been so real and absolute, seemed in fact purely clairvoyant.

He pulled into the driveway of his house—his house, that he had built with his desires, his beliefs, his love. Rosemary lifted the curtain at the window over the sink. Already he could smell supper, roast chicken, he thought. He hesitated, his hand on the door. And what was that all about? he asked himself, secure that the vision's power would be broken now that he was safely home. He got out of the car and went inside.

In the dining room Susan was setting the table and in the front room Jill and Mark were watching a tape of *Honey, I Shrunk the Kids*, shrieking at an especially exciting part. In the kitchen Rosemary was bent, looking into the oven. The last line from Yeats popped into his head: "Anarchy is loosed upon the world."

Dizziness struck him, he put out his hand to steady himself against the wall, but the house seemed to lurch and darken, and, for an instant, he recognized around him the chaos from Todd McKenzie's paintings.

Dennis Cooley

✦

small light from our window
swish of blown rain
there is something flannel
    & warm blankets
soft gurgle & drip

    drip drip something
    in us too i suppose
        leaking, lacking maybe

falls on the spots mellow
as a saxophone its wetness & as achingly
    beautiful philip the wet
    yellow ribbons the sounds
    wound round us a bowl &
    smell the earth smell
    —plums, or is it musky

    window a great emptiness
    behind it blind as a mirror
    when no one is home

that's it then isn't it
the garden we were promised
we would promenade in
an emerald brooch pinned there
on the chest of the world
told we once strolled in
happy as pups with the mother
loved and were loved

and then this poppy
its wick in wind flickers
a red bright as lipstick
/brighter
its wicked flesh

how the petals feel
the inside of peach
skin when it is peeled
inside your face you reach
your finger into run over
veins in your mouth
it rains in your mouth
the wet silk words

they are parachutes, fail to open
fall swiftly through the air
between us slippery and crash
and you sometimes touch at
night you actually touch

a poppy blown out over night
red on black felt

felt our lives swaying
on the dry sticks
each day beneath us we have
clung to tried to squeeze spring from

all the songs that stick in our throats
black birds clicking the sky open & shut
little specks of blood on our wings
the songs where we have
scraped them
,flying

me holding your hand holding back
we walk, slide the bank
hard to keep our footing
from falling in

slippery smell cattle have
stirred & punched holes
& then we hear it

noise & froth of water
black vein in earth
how quick it is & fast
& the coarse snow

air cool, cold to the touch
your hand so cold where you touch
& the grass long & full of dust
quick warmth on your breath
the haste

weight of our clothes
dumbness of buttons
quickenings we fumble

this clumsy uncoiling
our unoiled bodies in spring

rumbling when the train
passes overhead its heaviness
steaming in mist my ears
sound of blood rumbles in them

a certain muskiness a numbness
in us as we leave

the bare willows wreckage of reeds
a crow calls in disapproval
his black robes the poplars

climb out of our love
something sluggish at the bottom
winter not yet toppled by spring

everything we leave behind
the steep ravine the dark
water the stones
snow still on them

skirt wet & heavy with mud

never planned it this way
though there must be
those who would say yes
yes of course you have
this is what you wanted, all along

never wanted this though you must think so
must wonder what is it makes me
draw back in your garden from sun & wind

how is this place planted between us
so dried so hot it hurts
your feet when you walk

how this space is so desolate
so white without green words
or red & yellow ones bright in wind

a field of snow in blossom
a whole section of sorrow
and through it you & me

drifting

,drifting

dry ice in the wrong season

✦

the morning after
it is clear and bright
so bright you could see
forever it seems
only your eyes hurt
the whole world coated
the whitest white
Jan 31 & 30 below
a wedding cake
someone could have smeared

snow squeaks when you walk
then the joy the foot
warmer under the robes
the world coated with cold
you can see forever

& later that day
we are on our way
back from the Benson parish
Philip and I ride up over
land around us turning blue
stark & blue as electricity
night close that close
everything seems
to have shut & perished

the Harneys' rise horses snuffing
harness jingling so clear
it could be the beginning of the world
the runners break the crust
so bleak so cold now I
could weep almost for loneliness

I was thinking we could stop
at the Lennochs' for a cup of tea
yes Philip I would like that
that would be nice

something in me frozen
so big it could be a mastadon

and then over the crest
the sudden sprawl
off to the right
the red & white
the double shock
a wagon, old cart,
high narrow sides
tipped   in the ditch
a dozen cattle legs in the air
lying there like spilled toys
all those cattle frozen solid

hits me so hard
I will never forget this
never think of it without
the sense of
when you are skating &
suddenly you fall your head
bangs on the ice
your head ringing
so loud it hurts

don't you see philip don't you see
it is starting to come
out of my face out of my hands
for gods sake philip

all the murdered faces
the splotches muddy as mustard
the way it rains their faces
run all over our hands
& we can't get it off

the world was beautiful
                    once
don't you remember
        it was   almost

    & we were too philip
            we were too
you said we were
        you did philip
                you did
    & we were

            wish you could see
            my face is nearing
        the far side of the moon

why don't you say something
look why don't you look philip why
don't you touch me   once even

say this to him
age is coming
out of my face
& then it is over
it is all over
my face
it is all over

by the gosh i just waltzed him
right clean through the prairie
just as smart as you please
no if's and's or maybe's
right straight through the eyes
hopping all round us
faster than frogs in rain
snappy as buttons popping off

boy oh boy we were going
to set the world on fire
the prairie too if i had
anything to say about it

is that right i say
is that right

look he says look at this

clump in his hand
his hand open
the lump on it

stands there hand out—
the wind this steady steady wind
sturdy as Mrs. Wenderby's outhouse
blows every day all day without end
sometimes from the north the south
the east today it's from the west
it doesn't waver never lets up

look he says & you watch the wind
poking away chip chip chip
the clump disappearing in his hand
as if a hen were feeding
dirt trailing off that lump
you'd swear it was a lump of coal
a coal oil lamp the smoke coming off

sun so loud with heat
our lives are X-rayed
into grief

only it isn't it gets smaller
& smaller & then he crushes
& opens & then even the dust
's gone blown off as if
it were powdered blood
his hand drained dry

& then his hand begins to go
little bits of skin rip off & then
more & more the skin in shreds now
blows off in wind till it's only bone

perfectly white perfectly dry
the hand begins to shine
where the wind rubs

look he says look

& you do you look up
through the windy glass
you spot them trillions & trillions
grasshoppers high on a high hot wind
the terrible beauty of their noise
windy as birds as shrill

somewhere in a theater called the Rex
Shirley Temple lisps & twinkles
here they blacken the sky in their passing
the whole earth broken out under
us shaking us lighting lanterns all day long

all night long the terrible heat
when the winds would run low at last
the silent screams we take to bed
turn our cavernous & windy heads on
instruments waiting for music
cataracts of blood going through
all the wrecked music there

& then   the trestle over the creek
or once was a creek   the sound
the long long whistle   a train
always at night   you hear it
the long lonely sound   it plays from you
it plays   for you
gets into you   a thistle you pull
hollers   & your blood
answers back

on its way   to lovely names
to wet places   peaches   streams
that lonely whistle   every night
on its way   to somewhere
on its way   to loneliness

Lorna Crozier

Living Day by Day

I have no children and he has five,
three of them grown up, two with their mother.
It didn't matter when I was thirty and we met.
There'll be no children, he said, the first night
we slept together and I didn't care,
thought we wouldn't last anyway,
those terrible fights,
he and I struggling to be the first
to pack, the first one out the door.
Once I made it to the car before him,
locked him out. He jumped on the hood,
then kicked the headlights in.
Our friends said we'd kill each other
before the year was through.

Now it's ten years later.
Neither of us wants to leave.
We are at home with one another,
we are each other's home,
the voice in the doorway,
calling *Come in, come in,*
it's growing dark.

Still, I'm often asked if I have children.
Sometimes I answer yes,
sometimes we have so much
we make another person,
I can feel her in the night
slip between us, tell my dreams
how she spent her day. *Good night,*
she says, *good night, little mother,*
and leaves before I waken.

Across the lawns she dances
in her white, white dress,
her dream hair flying.

Canada Day Parade

Two days later and I've turned the parade
into a story I tell over drinks. Start with
my favorite part, the band from Cabri,
the whole town marching, children
barely bigger than their horns,
old men and women keeping time. Then,
riding bareback, four Lions' Ladies
in fake leather fringes,
faces streaked with warpaint, not one
real Indian in the whole parade.
Finally the Oilman's Float, a long
flatbed truck with a pumping machine,
a boy holding a sign saying "Future Oilman,"
beside him a girl, the "Future Oilman's Wife."
I tell my friends it was as if I'd stumbled
into a movie set in the fifties, that simple
stupid time when everyone was so unaware.

That's my story about the parade,
three parts to the narrative,
a cast of characters, a summing up.
I don't mention my father
sitting beside me in a wheelchair.
Out of the hospital for the day.
My mother putting him in diapers.
In the fifties he wouldn't have been
here beside us but somewhere down the street,
alone and cocky, drunk or about to be.
Or he'd have been racing his speedboat
at Duncaren Dam, the waves
lifting him and banging him down,
a violence he could understand,
that same dumb force raging inside him.
I won't describe my father
in his winter jacket, his legs covered
with a blanket in the hot light
bouncing off the pavement,
the smell of ammonia rising from his lap.

The day after the parade mom called
to say she saw us on TV.
When the camera panned the street
it stopped at us. "Not your dad," she said,
"they just caught the corner of his blanket."
As if he wasn't there.
As if he'd disappeared,
his boat flying through the air,
the engine stalled,
the blades of his propeller
stopped.

Inventing the Hawk

She didn't believe the words
when she first heard them, that blue
bodiless sound entering her ear.
But now something was in the air,
a sense of waiting as if
the hawk itself were there
just beyond the light, blinded
by a fine-stitched leather hood
she must take apart with her fingers.
Already she had its voice,
the scream that rose from her belly,
echoed in the dark inverted
canyon of her skull.

She built its wings, feather by feather,
the russet smoothness of its head,
the eyes hard and bright as beads
in that moment
between sleep and waking.

Was she the only one
who could remember them?
Who knew their shape and colors, the way
they could tilt the world with a list of wings.
Perhaps it was her reason for living
so long in this hard place
of wind and sky, the leafless trees
reciting their litany of loss
outside her window.

Elsewhere surely someone was drawing
gophers and mice out of the air.
Maybe that was also her job,
so clearly she could see them.
She'd have to lie here forever,
dreaming hair after hair,
summoning the paws (her own heart
turning timid, her nostrils twitching).

Then she would cause the seeds
in their endless variety—the ones
floating light as breath,
the ones with burrs and spears
that caught in her socks
when she was a child,
the radiant, uninvented blades of grass.

Country School

Inside the schoolhouse,
windows boarded up, the last day's
numbers remain on the slate
and the strange letter x.
It is alive and numinous
in this room without children.

A mother raccoon walks down the aisle
between the wooden desks
like a teacher checking sums.
Above her in the roof her little ones
wait for their lessons.

This is the hour for geography
in the classroom, the hour of
maps and names. She will teach them
how far they can travel before
the farm dogs pick up their scent,
and the shortest route to home.

What she will do when it is the hour
for poetry is unknown.

The cloakroom empty,
the bookshelves furred with dust,
on the blackboard the x
glows like the eyes of an animal
when it looks out of darkness
toward any kind of light.

Cleaning Fish

Dad, a little drunk, every summer Sunday
brought home a pail of perch
late in the evening like a prize (small,
but the tastiest fish you'll ever eat)
as another man might bring
a box of chocolates or
a rose.

Mom, who had spent the day alone
with me, sat on the back step,
mad as she could be
and gutted them, scraped
the scales with a Coke cap
nailed to a stick (he said
he didn't know how
to clean them right,
he'd lose the meat and keep
the bones)
I swore I'd not do that
for anyone.

Mom's hands became more fish
than flesh,
from fingertips to elbows
gloved in scales
as if she'd dipped her skin in sequins
and a little blood to make them stick.
Dad sat behind her
nursing his last warm beer,
the only sound the *swhitchh*
of Mother's scraping.

I stood off to one side
in my young girl's rage,
inventing what I'd say to them,
wanting so much
a different childhood
and swearing I would never be as unhappy
or alone as they,
believing then
I'd keep every single vow I made.

Mid-Summer Morning Run

The blue spruce all lean
in one direction. Without philosophy.
Nothing to push them this way or that
except the wind. Such a perfect
consensus! Beyond the shelter belt
some farmer planted forty years ago,
wheat rolls to the horizon and doubles back,
each kernel the soul of one newly dead
resting in the field as an animal will rest
before it heads for home.

The road I run borders the monastery.
Ahead of me a black man walks,
reading a book. Monk or not,
it's hard to tell. He must be
from a warmer place, he wears a jacket
and a red wool cap though it isn't cold.
I hope he's a missionary come from
far away to make us pagan. I am ready
to be fox or wild cat, to lift like
a crow into the high blue boughs,
my nest of sticks dancing in the wind.
I am tired of two feet, sick of death,
the sounds we make to give the world
its human shape.

              Oh to be a tree,
to lean in one direction,
to know the sky the way a tree
knows it, halfway to heaven, inarticulate,
the dead among the green wheat
holding their tongues.

On the Seventh Day

On the first day God said
Let there be light.
And there was light.
On the second day
God said, *Let there be light,*
and there was more light.

What are you doing? asked God's wife,
knowing he was the dreamy sort.
You created light yesterday.

I forgot, God said. *What can I do
about it now?*

Nothing, said his wife.
But pay attention!
And in a huff she left
to do the many chores
a wife must do in the vast
(though dustless) rooms of heaven.

On the third day God said
Let there be light. And
on the fourth and the fifth
(his wife off visiting his mother).

When she returned there was only
the sixth day left. The light
was so blinding, so dazzling
God had to stretch and stretch the sky to hold it
and the sky took up all the room—
it was bigger than anything
even God could imagine.
Quick, his wife said,
make something to stand on!
God cried, *Let there be earth!*
and a thin line of soil
nudged against the sky like a run-over serpent
bearing all the blue in the world on its back.

On the seventh day God rested
as he always did. Well, *rest*
wasn't exactly the right word,
his wife had to admit.

On the seventh day God
went into his study
and wrote in his journal
in huge curlicues and loops
and large crosses on the *t*'s,
changing all the facts, of course,
even creating Woman
from a Man's rib, imagine that!
But why be upset? she thought.
Who's going to believe it?

Anyway, she had her work to do.
Everything he'd forgotten
she had to create
with only a day left to do it.
Leaf by leaf,
paw by paw, two by two,
and now nothing
could be immortal
as in the original plan.

Go out and multiply, yes,
she'd have to say it,
but there was too little room for
life without end,
forever and ever,
always, eternal, *ad infinitum*
on that thin spit of earth
under that huge prairie sky.

Alan Davis

Growing Wings

Diane stopped using her full-length mirror when the small white feathers on her back were large enough to see from across the room if she twisted in her nightgown like a dancer. Closeup, the feathers were invisible, the angle of vision all wrong, so she turned the mirror around and stared for hours at its black paint. She also made regular retreats to a large utility closet full of baggy flannel shirts and large woolen socks. In class, sitting against the back wall, she wore a faded gray trenchcoat to hide the feathers, but her teacher, Mrs. Hanes, often made her hang it up in the coatroom.

She stared at a waterstain above the classroom door. Jamie, who always sat next to her, leaned close and whispered something. She failed to respond to him or to a question from Mrs. Hanes. "Pay attention," the teacher said. Diane lowered her eyes to the worn linoleum, pockmarked with swirling wormlike scratches. *We should learn not to be aware of ourselves,* she had read that morning in her sister's spiritual notebook, *to no longer have ideas, but to simply live what we are.*

"Diane, redeem yourself. What's the theme of *Lord Jim?*"

Her pennyloafers scraped circles on the tiles, a muffled rhythmic whisper. *You tend to interpret everything, an internal conversation goes on always in the mind.* She repeated Melinda's polished phrases for the comfort. *You must open yourself to the possibility of not-thinking, or meditation, as it's commonly called.*

"Diane!"

Jamie poked her gently. She looked up. My sister often wore purple, she thought; it's very spiritual. Maybe I should dye the coat.

Mrs. Hanes got the students writing. "Come with me, Diane." In the principal's office the steady hum of an air conditioner sounded like the whisper of shoe leather on tile and she thought about the Salvation Army store. Her mother would be scandalized to know how much time she spent there, off the beaten path her classmates followed to school, but it was comfortably musty with a smell of wool and mothballs. The woman at the store always let her sit quietly, often next to a wheezing air conditioner on its last legs, and she would listen to Melinda's voice. *We see what we want to see. We don't see things as they are. We have to discipline ourselves, watch the motes of dust in the sunlight, learn how to put such discipline into effect.*

Sometimes the woman gave her a glass of milk. "You ever talk, sweetie? Or do you just sit and think?"

For the first time Diane told someone. "I'm growing wings."

"Oh. Well, that's good, I suppose."

"I need an overcoat. Do you have one?"

"Oh, I think we might." The woman smiled and moved away with her sweet smell of Feen-a-mint. She fitted Diane with a coat a size too large. "It only costs a dollar today, wings or not. A special."

A hand placed itself gently on her shoulder. The principal. "Don't you listen, Dee?" He guided her to the counselor's office, his hand still on her shoulder like a small friendly animal. "I'm to leave you with Mrs. Esposito, to have a talk."

The door closed. "Hello, Diane."

A pause. "Hello, Diane."

A longer pause. "Well, we don't have much to say today, do we?"

The Universal Law resolves everything, but there is always a tendency to be impatient, Diane thought, still feeling the warm weight of the principal's hand.

Mrs. Esposito adjusted a small gold pin on her tweed jacket and shuffled through a manila folder. Violet nail polish, Diane thought. Why did she choose that color today?

"Now, let's see. You were just here, when? Last week? Yet here we are again, and you're still wearing those silly clothes. What's the story?"

Diane leaned forward. "Is something the matter with your eyes?"

"My eyes?" Mrs. Esposito picked up a small mirror. "My contacts, maybe? They seem okay, but let's look." She closed her eyes and gently massaged each eyelid. "How's that?"

"Better."

"Hmmm. Well. Tell me, how much time do you and your mother spend together? Does she have much time for you since your father and sister went away?"

Experience is a flash of lightning in a sky filled with dark clouds. She visualized the words as they appeared, neatly copied in her sister's elegant script.

"Dee? Did you hear me? What's the story?"

Diane smiled. "I'm fourteen years old." She held up both hands, fingers spread wide. She closed her hands and then displayed four more fingers, two on each hand.

"Yes, I know." Mrs. Esposito folded her hands over the notes and waited.

"It's my mother. You're right."

"Yes? What about her?" The counselor motioned for the girl to continue. "You can tell me, Dee. You can say anything. Nothing gets past these doors. I'm safe as a bank."

"Well . . ."

"Yes?"

"Well, my mother . . . Look, I don't know how to say this, Mrs. Esposito. But Mother, well, she eats tennis balls."

Mrs. Esposito's face reddened.

"It's the truth." Diane crossed her heart. "It's driving me bananas. But what can I do?"

"What do you mean, 'eats tennis balls'? What's that supposed to mean? Does she spend a lot of time at her club?"

"No, just what I said. She uses ketchup, mustard, sometimes a slice of onion. And on the *good* china, Mrs. Esposito. Can you believe it? It's disgusting." She pointed to the telephone on the desk. "Please call her right away and tell her to stop."

As she walked through the empty hallways, classroom voices discussed dangling modifiers and the Civil War. Words filtered into her awareness and fell away to vague murmurs. Drone City, she thought, and looked up. Sorry, sister, I'll get serious. Then she giggled, remembering the expression on the counselor's face.

Her trenchcoat and floppy hat waited in Mrs. Hanes' classroom. She overcame a desire to feign sickness or maybe just go home and settled instead for the comforting silence of the lavatory. The low hum of fluorescent lights, the coziness of dull porcelain and laminated particle board stalls made this the one place where she could stop thinking without fear of reproach. *They've told me I won't have to come back here again. This is the last time I'll have to go through this.* The words had the graininess of chipped marble, as though written on the wall before her. She stretched and turned to the mirror, twisted her neck and noticed how her flannel shirt bunched up near the shoulder blades.

"What happened in the office?" Jamie asked on the walk home. "They didn't kick you around, did they?"

There was a layer of sky above the one where most people stopped looking. She always had at least one ear cocked in that upward direction. I'm becoming better, she thought, at walking towards each moment without interpreting anything. But if I don't listen with discernment, I'll miss Melinda's calling when it comes. She saw Jamie frown. "Are you happy?"

"Huh?" Jamie shrugged. He looked down at his feet. "I guess."

"You ever pay attention to the way you walk?"

"Huh? I don't know. Not really."

"You ought to."

"I guess. You don't, um, pay attention sometimes." He stared down the street to her house. "By the way, you want to walk to the park before we go home?"

"No. Not today. I don't have time. Thanks, though."

"Oh. Huh. What else do you have to do?"

"I grow wings." She looked at him appraisingly.

"Oh. Wings, huh? I grow hair." He smiled.

"Well, goodbye, Jamie," she said when they reached her house. "Thanks for walking with me."

"Did you wink at me?" he asked.

She giggled. "Are you happy?"

"Sure. I'm glad you winked. Didn't you wink?"

"It doesn't matter. See you later. Be happy."

The sounds of dusk became clear, as though traveling across water. Diane sat on the front porch, her feet propped on the railing, leafing through Melinda's notebook and eating a banana sandwich. Next door dinnerware came from the cabinet and much later clattered in the sink. Eyes closed, she saw her sister talking in a slow hypnotic voice about the long spiritual struggle to leave behind the chains of the world, to climb cold mountain slopes. The dreamy voice brought Diane to the edge of trance, but willing her sister's appearance was more difficult. A car door slammed. Chords of practice exercises started up behind lacy curtains across the street, and then voices in the drive. Her mother stepped onto the porch, holding an unlit cigarette. "Hello, kiddo. You get something to eat?" No reply. "Jack and I are going to a movie. You want to come? It's a Burt Reynolds thing, a romantic comedy. But we've got to leave soon to make it."

"Okay. Have a good time. Don't eat too many tennis balls."

"Huh?"

"You better take it easy on the onions, Mother."

"Sometimes you're too silly to believe." She puffed on the unlit cigarette. "I don't have bad breath, do I?"

"Only when you frown, Mother." She riffled the pages of the closed notebook, still carrying a faint suggestion of patchouli. "Mother. Did Melinda ever grow wings?"

"Huh?"

"Wings on her back?"

"Wings? What are you saying, kiddo?"

"Wings, Mother. White, with feathers. Flap flap." She dangled her arms to illustrate.

"I still don't understand." She tapped her cigarette on the porch railing. "Stay in the real world, kiddo. It's all we have these days. Right?" She glanced at her watch. "Hey, you sure you don't want to come see Burt Reynolds?"

"What do you mean, 'the real world'?"

A large dog, fenced in, barked fiercely at a passerby. It was Jamie, shuffling past. He waved feebly and put his hands in his pockets, shoulders slumped. The car door slammed, her mother and Jack drove away. Alone, she realized how much she missed Melinda, whose presence always calmed her, like Sunday mornings stroking the veneered pew in church, daydreaming through stained-glass windows, absent-mindedly mouthing hymns. Across the street curtains parted briefly to reveal the wistful face of the young piano student. *All actions should be spiritual manifestations. If approached with the right motivation, it is fine to have all sorts of actions and experiences, even distractions, but not to attach to them.* Diane smiled. Maybe the girl secretly flapped her arms like wings, became a black crow and flew, squawking.

She lay on her bed. Were her own wings a sign from Melinda? Or rather, what kind of sign? Maybe she too had lived many lives, and had to be here only this one last time. In the light of a single candle shadows played on the ceiling. An owl chased a pumpkin, the owl became a cactus-flower, the cactus-flower became a pumpkin. The thunder of an airplane turned on car headlights that slanted through the window, illuminating a hanging fern, which in turn shed a tangle of waving fingers on the ceiling. A huge brown bird wearing her overcoat grabbed her. She fell into Jamie's lap, he kissed her, she reached up, touched her sister's lips. And woke, thirsty, uncomfortable, back aching, on the verge of tears. Don't think, she thought, and blew out her candle. There were places, she decided, remembering her wings and turning to her side, where she wasn't ready to go. One of Melinda's books, *Spiritual Initiation*, urged the apprentice to maintain detachment, discrimination, discernment, the three keys to interior serenity.

But she couldn't relax. Why did dreams of flying frighten her so? Why did Jamie, in her dream, become Melinda? Was she ready for wings?

✦ ✦ ✦

"Go to the counselor's office for your appointment," Mrs. Hanes said several days later. Distracted by Jamie, Diane stared at the floor, where a black ant made its deliberate way to a crumb.

"Young lady!"

She grabbed her coat and hat as she left.

✦ ✦ ✦

"Dee, please take off that ridiculous hat," said Mrs. Esposito.

"If you take out your eyes."

"How can you hear me with that stupid thing on?"

"Excuse me. What did you say?"

Mrs. Esposito lit a cigarette. She wore a neatly tailored suede jacket, dark green, which Diane wanted to caress. "You can be so sweet," she said after a long puff, "but you're in one of those moods, aren't you? What's the story?"

"There's nothing to be done." Diane stared into swirling smoke. "There's nothing to be done and nowhere to go."

"That's a ridiculous thing to say, isn't it, Dee? I mean, where would we be if we all thought that?"

"Nowhere."

"Exactly. Nowhere. We can't give up, can we?"

"You don't understand."

"Well, maybe not." The counselor stubbed out her cigarette. "You know, Dee, you haven't had much to say to me. Have you? Melinda died last summer and we still haven't talked about it. Is there anyone else you talk with?"

Diane touched her forehead. "What does this have to do with anything?"

"I don't know, maybe a lot. It depends what the story is." She reached across her desk. "Take this glass of water, for instance. I would say it's half full, but someone else might say it's half empty."

She sipped water and cleared her throat. "Look, Dee, it's not nice to have a father or sister die, much less both, and especially when it happens all of a sudden. I've had that happen."

"You had a sister die?"

"Well, no, I was an only child, but my father died when I was twenty, and my mother not so long ago." She stroked her chin. "They were sick, granted, and we expected them to go, but that didn't make it easier." She picked up a ballpoint pen and clicked it. "I only want to help. If we can monitor these automatic thoughts you have, maybe we can figure out some sort of rational response. Your thoughts affect your feelings, and then your feelings control your thoughts. It should be the other way around."

Diane breathed deeply. "What makes you think I need help?"

Mrs. Esposito leaned forward. "The way you get sometimes. The way you are right now. The way you react to my questions. You do want to talk, don't you?"

Suddenly Diane pulled her floppy hat over her eyes and lowered her voice an octave. "I have the trenchcoat. Don't you think I should ask the questions? Where were you on October 15th?"

"Come on, Dee. What's the story? Let's get down to brass tacks."

"Okay. You smoke cigarettes. Aren't you afraid of cancer? Think about it."

Mrs. Esposito smiled tightly, pulling back her lips into a line, one ready to spring from her face. She glanced at her watch. "Of course. You're right. I should give them up. Anyway, it's time for the bell. You think about it too, okay, Dee? We'll keep seeing one another for a while, or maybe we can find somebody else to help."

"Did you hear me in class?" Jamie asked.

"No."

"There's, um, a dance tomorrow night. It's in the gym. Want to come?"

"No. I don't think so. But thanks for asking, Jamie."

"You don't like dances?" Jamie kicked a divot out of

somebody's lawn. "Me neither. What I mean is, what else do you have to do? I mean, we can do something else."

She picked up a leaf and pressed it carefully into the pages of her book. "I told you. I grow wings." Why was she telling him again? It was secret.

"Oh." Jamie frowned. "That's interesting. And I told *you*, I grow hair. You know we all have the same amount of hair? Only some of us have it inside our heads and some of us outside."

Diane laughed. "That's funny, Jamie." He glanced at her and she giggled. "You don't believe me?"

"Oh, sure. Can I see?"

"No. Definitely not. Why you have to see? You can't take my word?"

"Yeah, I guess. But I let you see my hair."

"Let's forget about it. You have expectations, don't you?"

"What do you mean?"

"Think about it."

"Why should I think about it? Why can't you tell me?"

"Are you happy?"

"How can I be happy when you won't tell me?"

"That's what I mean."

She tossed in bed that night, tried to lie still, but her body was taut, wings larger. And she didn't feel comfortable on her stomach. She turned on the bedside lamp and the curtains ruffled in a slight breeze. She listened for crickets, but it was too late in the year. *They've told me I won't have to come back here again. This is the last time I'll have to go through this.* The last time she saw Melinda, her sister had a load of books for the library. "I'll be right back," she said. "You wait up and we'll make banana bread for the orphans."

Diane tilted her head quizzically. "Orphans?"

"You know," Melinda said, laughing, "the ones on the railroad tracks."

Oh, thought Diane, the cartoon we saw.

The memory made her angry. I've seen Melinda since then, she thought. Other people, no, but *I've* seen her. Staring at the well-thumbed notebook, she shook her head stubbornly and turned off the light. The library books, the last conversation, the way Melinda precariously balanced what she said and what she carried. At the funeral, clutching the book like a portable altar, deliberately impersonal, one of the few without tears, Diane was detached, even serene. Mourners descended upon her in black and dark greens. "They called for her," she told them. "The death was painful because she could learn something. And my father didn't feel anything." At the wheel, he had a heart attack, the car swerved across the highway's center stripe.

Come to me, she willed, sitting up in a half-lotus position. Instead, Melinda stood painfully vivid before the car with the library books. Okay, sis. I know things don't work that way, but give me a sign. In what form do you watch over me? Make yourself known, I will wait for you here. Her tongue swollen, she dragged herself to the bathroom for water. The light at the bottom of the stairs guided her down the hall, past her mother's empty bedroom, where two glasses glinted on a night table.

She gulped down the water and turned, to go back to her room. Instead, she slipped off her gown and opened the medicine cabinet over the basin. She took down a pair of scissors with blades the color of graphite. I'll trim my wings, she thought, beginning to cry. I'll have baby wings.

David Allan Evans

The Pond

For most of two back-to-back severe winters in his early teens he'd run home after school and get his skates, hang them over his neck and take off. He'd go down the bluff's steep creosote steps; if they were icy, he'd have to grip the icy railings all the way down. And then at the bottom he'd start out across the railroad tracks, walking past the roundhouse with its steaming engines inside, past the hobo house (an old caboose), to the baseball park. The pond—his winter secret, hidden by trees and a block from pavement—was beyond center field, next to the dump. Almost nobody went there in any season. It was too shallow and dirty for swimming, and he and his friends were afraid of broken beer bottles; and the bullheads, hooked with long bamboo poles, though good-sized and firm, had white spots on their yellow bellies and had to be thrown back in.

Once he found an old broom in his basement and took it to the pond. He found also, in the dump, sticking out of the snow, a grain shovel without a handle. If there was a thick layer of snow on the pond from the night before, he'd sweep a round space on the ice. If the snow was thicker, he'd shovel it off, then use the broom. Then he'd sit on a log and put on his skates. He had gathered chunks of wood, and sometimes he'd build a little fire to warm his hands.

In his figure skates he'd do his turns, spins, jumps and figure eights. All these he had watched once with his father at the Auditorium when The Ice Capades came to town. He loved to leap and turn halfway in the air and come down on his right foot, going backward, then leave his left leg out level and just coast.

He could spin like a top, his elbows clamped to his sides or his arms extended. If his skates were newly sharpened, he could not only feel but hear them biting into the ice as he moved in circles under an imagined spotlight, shifting his weight by turns from right leg to left, gliding on the inside or outside of the blades, as comfortable going backward as forward. He'd practice a move or a jump over and over, keeping track in his head of how many times, so that he knew he was improving.

The weather didn't matter. Below zero, sunny, overcast, snow, sleet, hail, rain. And the ice could be anything but crusty: diamond-hard-smooth, or slushy, or pocked and rough. If the world had been a giant skating rink, he would've tried to skate around it, sleeping and eating and whatever else without taking his skates off. He dreamed of turning pro, skating in The Ice Capades, or The Greatest Show on Ice.

One day his father, also a skater in his youth, told him that his (the boy's) grandmother had been born and raised in a Norwegian sea-coast town known for its skaters.

"Was she a skater?" the boy asked.

"She was a skater, and a very good one."

"What kind of skates did she have?"

"Racing skates. They all had racing skates."

And so he began to save his allowance, and he later talked his father into chipping in half. Soon after, his father came home with a pair of racing skates with fourteen-inch blades. He'd bought them at the Salvation Army store under the viaduct. The boy polished and buffed them to an exquisite black, and replaced the old black laces with new white ones, long enough to have to wrap around his ankles once, and then tie.

The pond was too small for racing skates—for wide, sweeping steps with one hand or both behind the back, leaning forward, crossing one foot over the other on wide, round, slow-motion turns, and flat-out sprinting which took a good five yards to hit full speed. He needed room. And so he had to use the town rink. But nobody else had racing skates, only figure or hockey. Was he trying to show off or something? And also, nobody could catch him when they played "I got it." The one who yelled "I got it" had earned it by catching and touching the one who "had it," and then taken off across the ice, all the others in pursuit, until somebody else "got it." But no hand could come close to his red parka with the flying hood if he'd had a decent head start of three or four quick steps. Not that he was as tricky and quick as Tom Boyd on figures. Boyd couldn't be caught either, unless the racing skates were after him in a straight-lined sprint.

Soon the others got tired of chasing him, especially when they always were caught. So he began to live three lives on the ice. After school for an hour or two, he was a figure skater on the secret pond, practicing to be a pro. He was a figure skater, too, at the town rink if he wanted to play games with the others, and he did. Then, for a third life, the best one: when it was too cold for anybody else to be there, or after or before hours, he was a racer, with nobody to race but his own long-footed shadow.

Then there was Dick Jenkins, who ran the warming house. This was an extra job, and the pay was minimal. He worked all day on the loading dock at Armour's, the packinghouse. In his late forties, he was grossly fat, and always wore a green De Kalb seed hat, gray overalls and black engineering boots, and he smoked a pipe, which he was constantly reloading and relighting. He was pleasant, dependable and helpful. If someone needed a shoestring or a sock or a band-aid, he could find it. If someone needed to borrow a pair of skates, or to trade for a bigger size, he could always find a pair.

Every school night—twenty above or twenty below—Dick was there to open the warming house at six p.m., and every weekend day at ten a.m. He knew the rules of the rink, but he let the kids do what they wanted to do as long as nobody got hurt. Pomp Pomp Pullaway and Capture the Flag were against the rules, along with Crack the Whip, which could be dangerous. But if there weren't too many on the ice and if they'd find a place on the south end for their game, and behave themselves, Dick would turn the other way. He wanted them to have a good time, and if they had to play games to have a good time, that was okay with him.

Just as a pitcher enjoys the crack of the ball in the catcher's mitt, and the horseshoe player the clatter of steel on steel, and the bowler the wooden thunder of a strike, so the boy enjoyed the sound of his blade tips scraping the ice as he glided across the rink. And, after a sprint from the far end to the warming house, the sudden shifting of the feet and sheer sideways skidding— learned also at the Auditorium from watching pro hockey—and the sudden, violent ice spray kicked up ahead of him as he came to a stop several feet from the warming house door.

That second winter—the coldest one in a decade, the old men said—often the boy was alone on the ice. Sometimes when he skated close to the warming house he saw Dick's head in the window, watching him. And then when he stopped and went inside to get warm, Dick would smile. Only once or twice did he praise him for his skating. But the boy knew he meant it, because he wasn't talkative. Mainly, he was just there, puffing Sir Walter Raleigh, shoveling chunks of oak and maple into the stove, and sweeping the skate-scarred wooden floor. The boy would lay his gloves on the stove and, if he was very cold, stand so close to the heat that his pant-legs would start steaming. Then he'd unzip his parka and sit on a bench for ten minutes or so. Maybe have a Coke from the machine, or a Milkyway candy bar. The two would sit in silence, warm against the crackling cold, the wind so fierce it made the windows hum. And then he'd zip up his coat, get his gloves and walk out the double door, clunking like a creature from an outer space movie, the skates adding several proud inches to his height. The very instant his second skate hit the ice, he was in a different world.

That was thirty years ago.

He had left Iowa shortly after his high school graduation and lived in southern California, working as a fireman and raising three children. He had been back only a couple of times, the last time four years ago for a class reunion, when he stayed out late enough to shut down a bar with his jock buddies, all drunk, all laughing with tears in their eyes over the past.

Then one day, a cold, windy Friday of another severe January, he was back again, with his wife, to see a good friend of hers who had recently moved back to Iowa and then, shortly after, conceded her life to cancer. When he could take no more, he left the hospital to have a look around the old neighborhood. He drove past the place where the ballpark had been; it was now a ready-mix company, its wooden fences replaced by strong mesh ones, with a belligerent-looking German Shepherd prowling around inside. He stopped on the shoulder of the road and parked, and walked the block to the pond. The wind bit his neck and bare head. The dump was still there. And so was the pond, but the trees were gone, replaced by frozen weeds. He leaned over the bank and looked for the spot he had once swept with a broom. The ice was covered with dirty snow, and on top of the snow was trash: some Styrofoam cups trapped in wire mesh, old shoes, cans, several truck tires, and, strangely, a rusted-out fender of a school bus.

He walked back to the car, this time with the wind, and got in and drove back across the tracks and up the bluff hill, to the ice rink. Now there was a Hy Vee supermarket taking up most of the vacant lot, and the rest was snow. The warming house was gone.

He parked in the store lot and walked across the street to the bar, Bill's Tap. When he'd been there last it was The Lodge. In his teens it had been Floyd's Tavern. He went in. The place was crowded, mostly with men wearing seed hats from the popcorn factory. He sat on the only empty bar stool and, when he got the attention of the bartender, ordered a whiskey and beer chaser. He downed the whiskey and started on the beer. Nobody looked familiar, though he saw a face or two that might have been related to some he had known. He checked his watch: 8:30. He had to pick up his wife in an hour.

He asked for another beer, put a dollar on the bar, and got up and went to the men's room. On the way back to his stool, he saw an old man sitting three stools away. His head, with a blue, tipped-up seed hat, was bent forward; he was staring as if into his beer glass and mumbling. He stepped closer and saw that it was Dick Jenkins. He tapped him on the shoulder. Dick turned around stiffly and looked at him.

"Hello, Dick, I'm—"

"I know you, Freeman. You're the skater."

"You remember me," he said.

"By God," said Dick, and he put out his hand and shook hands. "Here, get him a beer, Eddie," he said, motioning to the bartender, who was filling a glass.

"Okay," the bartender said, "but not for you." He took care of the other customer. Then he drew another beer, this one with a thick head spilling over, and set it on the bar, pushing it past the old man's hands, and picked up a crumpled dollar bill.

He took the beer. "Thanks, Dick," he said.

The bartender looked at Dick and then at him. "He's had his quota," the bartender said.

Dick waved him away, mumbling something, and sloshed what little beer was left in his own glass. He kept his eye on the younger man. He smiled; it was the same smile he'd seen in the warming house.

"By God I saw a lot of 'em, and you was the best," he said. Then he looked ahead again, his neck tired from turning, the smile gone. "By God, you could skate," he said, and raised his glass as in a toast, then tipped it to his mouth and swallowed the last of his beer.

"How've you been?" said the younger man.

"Oh, hell, I'm fine," he said, turning around again. "I'm fine. I retired, you know."

"I didn't know that." Then he remembered how old he was in the fifties. Dick must be around eighty.

"The rink ain't there no more," said Dick.

"I noticed there's a Hy Vee now."

"I retired. I used to work on the loading dock."

He sipped on his beer, standing close to Dick, who was shrunken and pale, whose gray overalls hung on him like a clown's clothes, or a man's worn by his child.

"You was the best," Dick said again. "By God." Then he leaned forward, his face almost touching his beer glass.

The bartender came over. "Maybe you ought to go home now, Dick," he said, speaking loudly. But Dick said nothing, only kept mumbling, the bill of his hat actually touching his beer glass.

"It was good to see you again, Dick," the younger man said,

and finished off his beer and set it on the bar. "Take care," he said. Then he left.

He walked out of the bar and across the street to his car. He stood there and looked at the place where the rink and warming house had been. The wind was picking up; it was almost too cold to snow. He pulled up the collar of his coat to protect his neck and ears, and then remembered the extended forecast of more snow by morning, and below-zero temperatures. But he would be flying home to California the next afternoon, so it didn't matter. Before he got too cold, he unlocked his car and got in. Driving out of the parking lot and heading for the hospital, he was starting to feel good, and he didn't know exactly why. But he knew for sure it wasn't just the whiskey and two beers.

Linda Hasselstrom

Prairie Relief

Human nature seems to dictate that we destroy what we most revere. For example, a sonorous prayer written by Reinhold Niebuhr of Heath, Massachusetts, for a Congregational church service in 1943 has become so popular it is widely abbreviated and misquoted. Dr. Niebuhr's original words were these: "God, give us grace to accept with serenity the things that cannot be changed, courage to change the things which should be changed, and the wisdom to distinguish the one from the other."

I've tried to be philosophical about differences between men and women—to truly accept what I could not change. For a woman who regularly rides a horse over a mostly treeless prairie, accompanied by males of varying ages and relationships, this demands some special reflection. I am as expert as a coyote in finding concealment where there seems to be none. When I locate any dip in the prairie, I usually stop my horse, leap off, unbutton my jacket, unhook my coveralls, and obtain relief from my full bladder. I'm quick as a coyote, too; given one uninterrupted minute, I can be mounted and mostly re-dressed when the males come into view.

But I confess I am sometimes guilty of envy when I glance ahead of the moving herd of cattle to see a man standing beside the pickup, gazing in apparent rapture at the changing colors of the Badlands in the east. His stance could mean any number of things: that he's looking at smoke in the distance, or cattle, or listening to the odd sound in the engine and diagnosing it. But I know he's not stunned by the magnificence; I know he's not lost in contemplation, forgetting his obligations to the world. I know what he's really doing. If I rode straight toward him at a gallop right now, by the time I got there, he would be smiling, turning toward me, perhaps remarking on the view.

Since I cannot change my own physical construction, I try to cultivate serenity, to see the difference as an advantage. When I am riding, my eyes move constantly, searching for a suitable spot with an absorbing panorama, or a wealth of nearby detail. Once dismounted, I look to minutiae. Electric blue dragonflies with a wingspan no wider than a quarter have perched on my hand; I've used a grass seed to lure ant lions. I have never found an arrowhead, but I return from most rides with a pocket full of seeds, or rocks with fascinating lines and whorls, or strange crystals embedded in their surfaces. Occasionally I use my belt knife to dig a healthy specimen of an unusual prairie plant, and tuck it in my pocket to be planted on my hillside. I position myself carefully in relation to plants that need extra moisture—an Indian turnip, or bluebell. I once heard of a man so careful of his resources that when he got cow manure on his shoe as he walked across the barnyard, he strode carefully so as not to dislodge it until he came to a bare spot, with only a few scraggly plants. Then he scraped the manure off where it was most needed. That man had the right perspective on his position in the world; he understood sustainable agriculture long before the term was coined. We are fertilizer, literally and symbolically.

Sometimes I regret modern dress codes which dictate that I wear jeans or coveralls instead of a dress while riding horseback. Oh, I know why women adopted pants, and the reasons are sensible; I'm not arguing for a return to crinolines and bustles. But when I'm in a rendezvous camp of black powder enthusiasts I realize the advantages of long dresses. A lady sitting on a log with her skirts spread around her might be communing with nature in any of several ways, and no gentleman would dare intrude. In the woods, I search for a spot that is not only concealed, but has a view, a mood, an ambience. The perfectly positioned log should offer adequate back support, and a rich supply of loose earth and dry leaves.

The prairie has no such equipment, but it does have

spectacular scenery. As I gaze at clouds making changing patterns in the sky, or at the rock outcrops behind which I am momentarily concealed, I realize that I am part of a long chain of human—and female—experience. Through millennia, women have felt the same envy, and have been unable to change the facts. We shrug, accept our differences, and transfigure the world in other ways. Perhaps we are the richer sex for the observations we have made while seeking relief. The female is the Earth Mother made flesh, and perhaps her differences should remind us of that. We are closer to the earth, more intimately involved with it than a male can ever be.

Coyote Laughs

I recently walked along a prairie creek with a hunter who was setting traps for beaver that had been cutting down young cottonwoods. Without the trees, the creek banks would erode more easily as cattle came to water, and smaller animals and birds would lose shelter and feed. Much as the ranch owner enjoyed seeing the quiet ponds the beaver built behind their dams, he believed the trees were of more use alive than dead.

"It's hard to know how to treat this land, especially with all that environmental talk," the rancher said. "I know I'm just taking care of it for the next generation. But I can't stand to lose a tree; it's too hard to grow them, and we never have enough. The beaver can take a hint and move up into the hills, but a dead tree will take twenty years to replace."

The hunter carried a rifle, because that particular rancher liked the coyotes in his neighborhood to stay nervous so they'd avoid his home and his chickens. The hunter made part of his living trapping beaver for ranchers along the prairie creeks; he checked his traps every day, and his careful sets rarely caught something else.

When coyotes were abundant, and their fur thick in winter, the hunter "harvested" some; he called it that, explaining that they were a renewable resource. "The only ones I can get with a rifle are the dumb ones, or the young ones that will start killing cats or chickens, find out how easy it is, and do it all their lives. The wild ones eat mice and moles, and insects if they have to. And clean up dead cows."

As we walked, he carried his basket of traps and the rifle, and I slogged along trying to remember how to use snowshoes. The first time I wore them out to get the mail at the highway, a neighbor stopped at the house to ask me what made the strange tracks. For some reason snowshoes were never adopted on the prairie; I scoffed, too, until my pickup stalled and I had to walk two miles home through hip-deep snow. I'd never have made it without the snowshoes. My husband grew up using them almost daily in Michigan, and got me a pair during our first winter together. He had used them so much they became second nature, but we seldom had enough snow for me to become really expert.

The day was sunny, warm enough to melt the edges of the snowdrifts, the sky clear and blue. The tall red grass gave the slopes of the hills a salmon pink cast. We were walking silently, not talking, when the coyote burst from a clump of brush just ahead of us.

I was behind and slightly above the hunter, and could look straight down the barrel of the rifle as he snapped it to his shoulder and fired. The bullet clipped the coyote's tail; the brush jerked. Then, almost too fast to see, the tail whipped to the right, and the coyote spun to his left and flew over the snow, diving into a gully just ahead of us. We ran after him, but he was out of sight when we rounded the bend. Directly in the center of our path was a willow tree, and a yellow stain.

"Not too worried, is he?" the hunter said, laughing, gasping for breath. "Even had time to leave me a message to show what he thinks of my shooting."

We followed him a little further, but we both knew it was futile, and we didn't care. Walking back up the creek, we found a few drops of blood and some long, silky tan hairs—the shot must have clipped the coyote's tail. I was glad he missed; I love the coyote's night song, his serious approach to rodent control, and his laughter at humans, so inadequate in his world.

"I'll bet he's sitting up there in those trees on the rim someplace, watching us and laughing," said the hunter. The next day, walking the rim, we saw where he'd curled up to nap until we went away.

Following a Cabin Cruiser in a Blizzard

Nose raised to the wind,
I'm headed west on Interstate 90.
No landfall in sight;
I couldn't even see
the last rest area I passed.
Snow thin as spray or blown salt
drizzles across my hood.
The car keeps drifting off course,
pulled and pushed by wind.
My sails are reefed, hatches battened down;
everything loose rattled to rest
when I skidded into the ditch.
On a sunny day I'll sort and stow it back.
For now my goal is somewhere I can't see,
a rocky shore hidden by clouds, wind, fog.

Occasionally a small, fast craft
appears off my port side,
shoots past me into white froth.
The car rocks on wind and asphalt waves.
I think I'm on solid land,
passing small farms with lighted windows
where farmers pace while wives fix dinner.
But my eyes see nothing but heaving white.
We prairie folks love these ocean metaphors;
long before the first college rose,
some cowboy tanned to leather by the sun
called my country the "sea of grass."
We're desperate for any kind of water.

The bowsprit lifts, points at sky;
waves thump under the hull,
crash on a reef of trees to starboard.
The flashing light of the truck
hauling the cabin cruiser
becomes a lighthouse,
a buoy warning of deep water.
I'm afraid to stop
the steady engine throb and step outside—
my foot might find nothing,
my body sink, my lungs fill
with salt sea water,
or blood.

Pennies for Luck

A heron flaps upstream, the color of fog over the river.
The bridge throbs under my tires.
I roll the window down, throw as hard as I can, listening.
I don't hear a ricochet;
the penny must have sailed past the bridge railings
dropping down, down toward the water.

I've been throwing pennies-for-luck
into the Missouri River for years.
Only today do I wonder what happens
when they fly out beyond the bridge rail heading for water.
Fish may leap for the sparkling lure
and die with pennies in their guts;
seagulls may snatch them in midair;
what kind of luck is that?
A news story I never see may tell of fishermen
mysteriously unconscious. "I don't know,"
he said, "I was fishing under the bridge
alone in my boat and it felt like someone
dropped a rock on my head."

One passenger didn't understand the ritual;
with both hands he scooped parking change from the
    dashboard
while I laughed helplessly. But he's an environmentalist;
he needed all the help he could get from the river gods.
Once a penny leapt back, spanging against the car door.
I drove with extra care that day.

Today I threw twice, for good fishing
where you are.

Bill Holm

Glad Poverty
The History of Two Poor Icelandic Women from Minneota

I come to the garden alone,
While the dew is still on the roses;
And the voice I hear, Falling on my ear;
The Son of God discloses.

Chorus:
And He walks with me, and He talks with me,
And He tells me I am His own,
And the joy we share as we tarry there,
None other has ever known.

—C. Austin Miles

I

Sara Kline was the most visibly poor woman in Minneota when I was a boy. Old, small, shriveled, hunched over, almost toothless, she wore the same black rags for years on end, the same black high-top tennis shoes with a dozen frayed knots in the laces, her stringy greasy gray hair covered with the same black scarf. Her stoop probably came from scouring the gutters with her poor eyesight for serviceable cigarette butts which she liberated from the cement or under the sidewalk gratings into her filthy cloth bag—a Minneota "bag lady" years before that language became fashionable.

But the strongest image of her poverty came not so much to the eyes as to the nose. Within twenty or thirty feet, her presence announced itself: a stale smell of unwashed damp rags, sweat, uriny underwear, rotted food in rotted teeth, old cigarettes, the fetor that rises off a mattress that should have been thrown away decades ago, the smell of the old and poor who have ceased to be able to care—whose vanity has atrophied out from under them.

I came from a family of big men, making my judgment of human size, particularly those out of memory, probably not trustworthy; but I remember Sara as half the size I thought a normal human. She was closer to the earth than she should have been. That proximity is not a bad metaphor for her whole life.

In the forties and fifties, Saturday was the night for open stores, shopping, visiting, cleaning up after a week of farm work, driving the pickup or old car down the gravel road to town, buying groceries, beer, bolts of material, haircuts, oyster shells for the chickens, Velveeta for the humans, gossiping while you sat on the warm car hood, going to Medart Debbaut's Joy Theater for Hopalong Cassidy, popcorn and Mr. Nibs. This was the midwest version of bright lights and urbanity. The town crinkled with crisp new bib overalls; the wind of a summer night lost itself in a labyrinth of sticky hair spray and died calmly away.

But Sara Kline was always there to remind you that this was not Norman Rockwell's America, not a Farm Bureau poster of contented, prosperous rural family life, that God, even if he were on duty at the moment in heaven, had not quite yet managed to make all things right with the world.

The Saturday night division of labor in the Holm house was this: my father said his obligatory hello's to whoever my mother thought necessary, and then disappeared into the Round-Up Tavern for whist, rummy, buck-euchre, beer, Camels, swearing, and male privacy; my mother investigated whatever bargains might have surfaced during the week at the Big Store, or Johnson's Red Owl Store, and exchanged her ritual information with other ladies who liked Saturday night chumminess; I tried to disappear into Hopalong Cassidy as quickly as possible, or find some gang of underage street marauders setting off to engineer themselves into parentless, thus more interesting, situations.

Before these rituals began, however, there came another and

sterner test. My father parked his dirty brown Dodge as close as possible to the Round-Up. This meant we passed Sara's light pole. She lived in a room back of a crumbling frame building on an alley behind the Round-Up. Minneota was then a town of broad front porches, picture windows facing the street, unshaded and unhedged front lawns, and chairs set on the grass in front of the house. An alley meant something to hide, a place to throw garbage, to piss, to be drunk, to quarrel, to smoke (if you were a teenager), to tell low jokes, a place for shame, for the poor, for strangers, for what did not want to be seen.

Children are constitutional xenophobes; it is their natural instinct to humiliate and abuse the crippled, the old, the ugly, the peculiar, the grotesque. Children love their own beauty and energy so much that they excoriate others for lacking it. Neither any of my contemporaries in Minneota nor I was unusual in that regard. The process of being made to feel guilt and shame for that xenophobia, thus stopping its progress, is called civilization. It is the first duty of parents.

Mine took their responsibility with what, at the time, I thought was an uncommon severity. They instructed me that I was never to pass Sara Kline without shaking her hand, greeting her courteously in Icelandic, and worst of all: bending down to kiss her on the cheek. Even as a young boy, I towered over her shrunken black figure. My mother coached me in proper Icelandic grammar, so that I would not commit the awful sin of using a male ending to address a lady. "Komdu sael og blessath, Sara," I would mumble, preparing myself for the smelly and humiliating ordeal.

She was always there, waiting on the sidewalk in front of the old barbershop and workboot store that shared the front of the ramshackle building. My father greeted her on his way to the Round-Up door; my mother chatted a bit in Icelandic, probably inquiring after Sara's health, and then it was my turn. With a feigned courtliness, I greeted, shook hands, kissed, all the time hoping that none of my classmates was watching this ordeal. Sara would tell me that I was a nice boy and getting so big with such fine red hair just like my mother's and then reach up and pat my cheek with her leathery, grimy hand. Then it was over for perhaps another week.

I had not, at the time, read the story of Jonathan Swift and the beggar woman outside St. Paul's Cathedral in Dublin. After preaching one Sunday on the subject of charity and humanity to the poor, he was making his way down the steps of his Cathedral still dressed in his ecclesiastical robes when an old beggar reached up her hand for alms. Swift looked down at the hand, then turned away in disgust. "She might at least have washed that hand," he is reported to have said, and so might I have said, if my parents would not have disowned me for saying it.

Indeed, Guttormur Guttormsson, the Icelandic minister in Minneota for fifty or sixty years, did not say it either. Like Swift, he was dean of a St. Paul's, but this smaller one was built of oak in 1895. He greeted Sara each Sunday at the door of the church with the same courtesy and, of course, the same impeccable Icelandic that he used for his most elegant parishioners. She was a regular church-goer, always arriving a bit late and sitting alone at the back of the church. She had, without intention, a private pew, and her fellow Icelandic Lutherans should be forgiven for not wanting to crowd her too closely. Guttormur's sermons were heroically long, and the church stuffy.

By the time I was a teenager, I had become a sporadic church organist, with a perch in the balcony where I surveyed the congregation, read D.H. Lawrence novels, and otherwise avoided being improved by lengthy discourse on the theology of sanctification and grace. I always carefully watched Sara while the collection was taken; she never failed to put her coin or two into the velvet dish full of silent paper, always letting go of them with a little regret, turning her head to follow the plate of money as it made its way down the aisle toward the pink painted Jesus.

Like many other old ladies, both rich and poor, she asked me to sing at her funeral, and I did. For Sara, I sang "Come, Ye Disconsolate" and "I Walk in the Garden Alone." She was cleaner in her coffin, brighter, paler, though even smaller, and, I think, happier. There was, as I remember, no family at all to sit in the mourners' pews, but, instead, a good many of the congregation who, of course, had known her well for three quarters of a century.

My mother was a great repository of stories and local history, a sort of village gleewoman, but she was always closemouthed when I asked her for the history of Sara Kline. "She was a poor woman, and her life was full of suffering," Jona said, "and children were always mean to her because she was dirty and odd-looking. You mustn't add to that; and when you see Sara always go out of your way to greet her respectfully in Icelandic and kiss her hello. She deserves . . ."

"Yes, yes, yes," I would interrupt this often chanted mantra, "but what *happened* to the poor woman that reduced her to such a god-awful life?"

"Her life was full of suffering, and you must always . . . ," Jona started again, making no progress at all in giving me the details of Sara's obviously dark checkered past.

I found out something of her past almost accidentally, long after both she and my parents were dead. Sara was buried in the Icelandic town graveyard a half mile south of Minneota. Most of the names on the stones there were normal, everyday names like Gislason, Hallgrimsson, Bjornsson, Guttormsson, Hrafnson, Jokull, but there were a few odd ones like Schram and Kline. Their oddness never occurred to me as a boy; I assumed that God had made certain that only Icelanders wound up in such a favored spot, and could be trusted to dispose of others elsewhere. But one day, I was walking through the cemetery with a family of distinguished and elderly Minneota Icelanders who knew everyone in the place, and addressed them by name as they stepped over their stones.

"Look at that," said Bjorn. "Someone mowed Skunk's grave, and planted flowers on it. It's better than the son-of-a-bitch deserves."

"Skunk?"

He pointed down to the grave of a man dead in 1945. "Why is his grave next to Sara's?" I asked.

"Didn't you know? Sara was his mother. She was a hired girl brought over from Iceland by old Schram. He was German by descent, not Icelandic, an old pirate of a merchant. One of his brothers got Sara pregnant, and then gave her nothing. He went back to Iceland. She was a poor ignorant girl, and raised her boy alone. He grew up to be a drunk, stole from his mother, abused her, finally died drunk."

"And his nickname was Skunk because . . ."

"It suited him."

The poor withered, unwashed body of Sara rose up inside me; I smelled the stale half-smoked butts in her bag, felt her leathery paw on my cheek again. This was the story my mother never told, the reason I was so punctiliously trained to treat Sara as if she were a countess. Quite enough had happened to her in this world, thank you very much, and she needed no more indignity on her way out of it. Civilization often consists not so much in knowing what to do the first time around, as in being intelligent and humane enough to try, without much hope, to repair the damages, or at least to offer some honest consolation on the second go.

Sara's poverty and misery were of the kind that could not be hidden. She had no resources to hide them anyway. She was not beautiful, she was not educated, and she was not endowed with the arrogant bravado and self-possession that sometimes get you through this world without either gift.

II

Just as Sara Kline could never hide her poverty, so my Aunt Olympia Vilborg Sveinnsdottir Holm Amundson Quamen could never show it. My father was the baby of a family mostly of sisters, and despite the fact that by the time I knew him he was a rough-spoken, gray-haired, burly man, he was pampered and bossed like a small boy by his three older sisters: Soffia, Dora and Ole. I loved them dearly as a boy, those three big kindly women, but Ole had me entirely in her thrall, as she did all men.

She was born in 1904, and I still own a photo of her as a teenager, taken in 1922. It shows her dressed in a gauzy light-colored dress that whips around her knees in the wind. She grins coquettishly straight into the camera. She is standing in front of the old Round-Up, a few Model T's parked in the background. She loved having her picture taken; she loved being watched and admired; she loved men, like Oscar Wilde, not wisely but too well; she probably loved the unknown cameraman taking the snapshot on the main street of Minneota, and flirted with him both before and after, and clearly during the picture. I would bet my last dollar that it was not a woman holding that camera, and no one who ever met Ole would bet against me.

She was not, I suppose, a beautiful woman by conventional standards; she was vengefully Scandinavian-looking. But then, how am I to judge? She was my aunt, and I was in love with her too, from the age of perhaps three onwards. It is enough to say that other human beings always found her attractive, and when she walked into a room full of strangers, she never failed to get her fair share of their attention. She had been, for part of her life, a beauty parlor operator, and never allowed anyone to see her less than well turned out. Her hair, elegantly snow white for the last fifty years of her life, was always "done"; her makeup was in place; her fingers were ringed, not expensively, but splendidly and gaudily like a Viking gypsy; her clothes were bright and silky, lavender and cream; Ole was no Puritan. And her Emeraude! It was, I imagine, dime-store perfume, but I smell it as I write this sentence. It is redolent of attar of roses, of ambrosia, of lavender, not of women but of movie goddesses, not of reality but of memory. After Ole sat in a room, it held her ghost in the curtains, in the cushions of the sofa and the chair, in the crocheted tablecloth, for hours, for days, I think, for years afterwards.

Probably much to her own daughters' chagrin, she loved little boys much more than little girls. My first memories of Auntie Ole were her visits to my father's farm. She swept into the small cold parlor, Emeraude trailing behind her, rings clanking like Cleopatra's tamborines, and hoisted her small fat bespectacled nephew into her lap. "And how's little Bill? You've got dimples just like your father used to have; and you're getting so big and strong! And how much do you love your old Auntie Ole today?"

How do you answer a question like this? I remember rashly promising to get rich when I grew up, so that I could buy my dear

Auntie Ole a fur coat. Her not entirely whimsical complaint to the universe and to any adult within earshot was that her old Persian lamb was moth-eaten and bare, and she could afford only fake coats, an unsatisfactory substitute.

The offer of the coat delighted her, and she then plunged into her second perennial request. "And you have such a beautiful voice, little Bill, you must promise me that you will sing 'I walk in the garden alone, while the dew is still on the roses . . .' at my funeral."

With violent protestation that she was never going to die, I would promise it, and then shift subjects as fast as possible. It remains one of my small gratitudes to the divinities of luck that I had to wait a very long time to make good on that second promise.

On the first, the fur coat, I failed. But then Ole never really expected men to get rich or to make good on their promises of wonderful gifts. Experience in that regard had been too unkind to her.

Her father, my grandfather, died of pneumonia when Ole was five, and her widowed mother raised five children with next to nothing, partly on the charity of better-off relatives. Ole married young, a handsome though none too prosperous local Norwegian farmer, and had her three children during the depression. Just when times might have improved for her, her husband died of epilepsy, and left her, like her mother, a poor widow with young children.

She moved to South Dakota, and opened a beauty parlor, assuming, I suppose, that beauty was the only skill that nature had left her to put money in the bank. But her bad luck continued. She turned out to be allergic to the chemicals she had to use, her Icelandic skin burst into fiery rashes, her blood pressure went up, and her temporary trade was finished. By this time, she had met and married her second husband, Earl, a carpenter and stone mason. He was the uncle I remember, a gruff, grizzled and likable man, a little Bogart machismo about him without Bogart's hand-someness. And he drank a little. . . .

And a little more as time went on, so that Ole found herself broke again. She was not, I suppose, a good manager of money,

and was at least partly to blame for her own troubles. Her health
began to give out in her sixties and seventies, though it was never
visible behind the disguise of Emeraude, rings, lavender dresses,
and a fluff of elegantly coiffed white hair. But when she was
widowed for the second time, she cracked, overdosed drastically
on her pills for various ailments, and she found herself confused,
almost comatose and broke. She involuntarily moved back to the
nursing home in her home town, Minneota.

By this time, I had moved back to Minneota too, and saw Ole
several times a week. As I approached my forties, I was a little
old to go through the old routine of crawling into her lap, but Ole
was not past her part in the charade. Despite the ravages of bad
luck, illness and poverty, she remained a good-looking woman.
Her vanity was intact. Emeraude was still on sale at the drug store,
and Ole's bottle was not empty.

The sun room of a nursing home is not a cheerful place, despite
the sun. Rather it is a sort of canyon floor, strewn with the
wreckage of great falls from the cliff, the bodies not yet quite
washed away by the river. Remnants of human beings sit strapped
into their wheelchairs, leaking on themselves, moaning in an
undecoded language, half asleep. Having known Ole in something like her prime, at fifty, I could see the ravages of her
experience in her face, in her talk, in the slight disarray of her
blouse, but in that room, even in her reduced grandeur, she was
not a client, but a countess come to visit the old, cheer them, and
scatter the largesse of her elegance. At core, she was still the old
Ole. She flirted. When a man walked in the room, twenty years
dropped off her, her eyes brightened, and she almost audibly
mumbled: "Here we go again!"

I knew she was not long for the nursing home when I came
one day and found her in a lively conversation with one of the
other inmates. The other woman was kidding Ole about being
broke, and in need of a man, preferably rich. "Why, Ole, old Steve
is ninety-two, owns three farms, and one of the nurses said he
could still get it up when she came into his room. He's the man
for you, Ole."

Ole said, "I wouldn't touch old Steve with a ten-foot pole if his ass was plated in platinum." Ole, for better or worse, married only for love. She was romantic to the end. Another day, I brought a friend, an out-of-town girl, to meet Auntie Ole. Ole told her funny stories about the old Icelanders. "What is an Icelander, Ole?" my friend asked. Ole paused, but not for long. "An Icelander, by descent, is forty percent Norwegian, forty percent Irish, and twenty percent traveling salesman."

Her wit was bawdy and vivacious, and it never left her. But neither did her complaining. Those she had no interest in charming, she blamed. Every magnificent character has her own darkness, even if we choose for a while not to see it.

One day, I went to see her, and she was gone. "Back to Sioux Falls," said the nurse, "and into a nice apartment building for old folks. Everybody dresses up fit to kill there."

"She'll like being among the rich," I mumbled.

"You know," the nurse mused, "I could never figure out why a woman as fancy as your aunt came back here. She was always so gracious and kind, but you could tell she was used to money. She was classy. Was her husband a banker?"

I think I fell to the floor in a fit of involuntary laughter before I could reply. "Ole was so poor her whole life that she often had no money to eat, went days without food because she was too proud to use food stamps. She had," I emphasized, "neither a dime nor a pot to piss in for over seventy years."

"Well, you never know . . . ," sighed the nurse.

Indeed, you never do. Ole blossomed in her last few years, found a lively boyfriend, a good dancer, but he up and died of a heart attack, so she found another one—a retired South Dakota real-estate agent. The two of them were inseparable and probably illegal, but Ole was Ole, and nearing eighty is no time to moralize. They lived together, had little spats, made up, rolled their eyes at each other, and generally enjoyed life.

But even long lives end. John died, and Ole's will to go on seemed to leave her. Eighty was enough. I went to see her a few days before she died. I walked into her hospital room and found her still Ole. Her hair was lovely, though she apologized for it.

"You should have warned me you were coming." She was wearing not a hospital robe, but a silk dressing gown, and there was Emeraude somewhere in the air. Solicitous as always about male comfort, she insisted that her daughter Emmy Lou and I walk her down to the sun room. "Damn fools in this place won't let you smoke in the room." I had been warned that she was having hallucinations—seeing people who weren't there.

The three of us sat in the empty room full of brilliant sunlight, not talking much. Finally, Ole said, "There he is again!"

"Who is it, Auntie Ole?"

"It's the little boy. He's there in the corner behind the curtains. He's following me; don't you see him?"

"Oh, Mother, there's no one there," said Emmy Lou.

"Well, if you say so. But he's there." Her angel of death was true to her character. It was a handsome boy. If a little girl had come, I think Ole would have refused the summons.

As I did for Sara, I wound up singing "I Walk in the Garden Alone" for Ole. The chorus was weirdly appropriate: "He walks with me, and he talks with me / And he tells me I am his own." Jesus as a gentleman caller was the only theological image that made any sense to her.

After the funeral, drinking coffee with relatives, I proposed that the scheme for Ole's funeral had been all wrong. She ought to have been cremated, and her ashes taken up in an airplane somewhere over the American west and dropped on a town full of lonely men. Many heads nodded in agreement.

An historian examining bank statements and indebtedness would probably not find much difference between Sara Kline and Auntie Ole. Yet in actuality, a whole universe separated these two Icelandic women. One sank under the weight of her poverty, and wore its visible signs like Hester Prynne's scarlet A; the other used up all her energy as a human to stay visibly afloat and buoyant, even though sea monsters had fastened their tentacles around her legs, trying to pull her under. The question of which poverty was more glad is not as easy to answer as you might imagine.

Robert King

At Reevey's Prairie

> July 6: We set sail, and at one mile passed a sandbar,
> three miles farther an island, a prairie to the north, at the
> distance of four miles, called Reevey's Prairie, after a
> man who was killed there.
>
> —Merriweather Lewis

Black-winged grasshoppers crackle up
from a ditch and settle into the brush,
rustling like old maps.

All the fine-rooted grass branching
the earth, its tough lace deep as the dead,
has been scoured clean

until the place is smooth farm now,
Reevey forgotten. We try to call the air
in our own language.

Lundgren's Grove. The Johnson Place.
Lost Woman Creek. Words fade
as if strong sunlight made them thin.

Soon wagons on the blank road
had no wood to mark the graves,
names evaporating like prayer.

Grasses move in sentences
we are afraid to understand,
or water running under winter ice.

Lewis is gone who named an island
Sunday for the day he passed it.
Sandbars rise and fall in seasons.

Along the river, the cottonwoods creak
like men shifting in their saddles
for a moment, for a moment stopping.

Old Lake Agassiz

We knew this valley was an ice-age lake
so we believed in centuries
when something swam in the air above our heads.
We have looked for bones in the fields,
for fossil prints, the way one looks
to the sky for God, trying to pick up
a history under our feet.

We are tired of gazing into the shallow furrows.
If anything is in this soft fill
it has sifted too deeply to find.

Now and then, toward an invisible shore,
the plow turns up a boulder blank as ice.
At the end of a warm spring day, we drag it
to one of the rocky heaps inherited
with the field, old monuments
to nothing but endurance.

We shuffle across the bottom toward the house,
the air washing against us,
dust circling our boots
with small whirlpools of milky light.

Late Harvesting

Autumn, and the children leave,
night edging in from the roads.
The pickers rattle down the rows,
digging at whatever was buried:
potatoes, sugarbeets, desire.
To reach the end is to return.

A wife rubs her eyes, slumps in the cab,
the conveyor throbbing against her.
Promises rise and pour into the bellies of the trucks.
Her husband bends to pull at the world,
dredging the dirt for roots the shape of food,
their centers white as a daughter's skin.

All they held has loosened, emptied out.
In bed, exposed and numb, they open up into sleep
the way fields wait in the cold. Their hearts
echo, something pumping in the earth.

Trees bow, the shape of stones around the farm.
Sons are marrying in the black ditches,
daughters giving birth in the hollows of rooms, listening
to voices across the fields, their own childhood
calling from the porch in the first language.

In the Northern Towns

we are familiar with absences.
The wind drops letters
from the marquee, making

nonsense of the show,
and snow drifts over the absent-
minded shovel.

The vacant lot
that held a house is rabbited
with tracks. Even

the river is always
leaving and the wrong direction.
Where would we end?

Soft, soft, the
skiers slide cross-
country in the park.

Walking with Father in Colorado

Everywhere I followed him back in time,
by the new reservoir, boards from flooded shacks
still floating up, or the convict cabins
where, the year of my birth, they cut a road
through pines that lost itself, the clearing
trash and bedsprings sinking into the grass.
My lessons were only hills of abandoned mines,
towns that shrunk into ravines, until one afternoon,

heading for a timberline lake early in the season,
he finally lifted me on his shoulders, his boots
breaking through the snow crust so my bones jarred
as if I were feeling what it was to walk
for the first time.

The lake was oval darkness
in a hollow of white. Its meltwater creek
would slow into the river through our town.
Fingers aching, I swirled up icy glints
of mica, pebbles of quartz, the rose of feldspar.
Dazed to the heart by the bright secrets
of beginnings I could not even tell myself,
I knelt and drank from the shining in my hands.

The Car at the Edge of the Woods

This is how it is done:
you drive the car up
to the edge of the woods and slowly
turn it on its side.

Parts spill from the engine,
sprout into garden patches,
a trailer, one tarpaper door.
The sky clouds over

chickens, bits of machinery.
Grass whispers comfort
around the metal: you have married,
have a child. The garden grows

a swing-set, seedlings of birch
stretch by the wreck, the windshield
crazes like new oil. Kids
slide into high school and talk

becomes gesture. Your wife's
skin toughens. She
begins to like fishing.
You sit together in the rain.

Last year's cattails ooze
like seat-stuffing, the swing-set
rusting to weed. Your trailer
has weathered the darkness of cloud

and looks like any stone,
though hollow, warm, inside.
You have driven your car to the edge
of the woods, left it there, and stayed.

The Girl in Valentine, Nebraska

The x-ray map of my foot lit up,
the doctor points to the thin line
fracture, already being healed
by calcium. We smile together
at the body's smooth successes.
All the way home I think how we
are covered over for the future,

remembering the small white scar
on the cheek of my first girlfriend,
the zigzag of a childhood accident.
When we kissed, I imagined feeling it,
excitement numbing my tongue.
She has been married thirty years,
a husband knowing everything about her

but the things I know that have disappeared,
loss blurred into loss. Near my home
the prairie ruts of famous wagons
grew vague and grassier each year
and on a sandstone bluff by the Laramie

I read the names of travelers needing
something to cut their lives into.
Passing my fingers over the flowered script
I felt stone rub into a gritty dust.
In the Deadwood Cemetery's oldest corner
I found a stone where "Mother" in white marble
weathered into a round dim word.

Years ago, in Valentine, a teenage girl
reached a rootbeer into my car, her sleeve
lifting from a pin-pricked amateur tattoo,
the infected scratch of a jagged heart
on her soft bicep, proud and sexy, swollen
in rebellion, doomed to be erased
by all her other lives and deaths.

How I Get Home Tonight

I turn north on 1, past my dad's old place, the land
as dark as the sky so I can only feel the hollow
in the trees his house has left. My headlights scald
the names off mailboxes as they blur by.

Ahead, a car rises and bears down, brights flaring,
heading toward a place to be I have passed.
I don't live here. We find ourselves by intersections;
I'm five miles south, two west, of home. I slow

for the short main street of Hanville where a girlfriend lived,
her ex-husband still at the bar with his new pregnant wife,
and ease out, gathering speed between the black plowed rows.

I could be traveling anywhere with this illusion
I am alone, tracing the latitudes of neighbors,
and this illusion I am not alone, not having lost
direction, but the purposes of direction.

A country road collides and I tackle a stretch
of gravel, the loose wheel thrilling in my hands.
The darkness widens, the radio drifts off course.
Something inside the earth loosens, floating up.

Just before the hill starts sliding into the river
I turn up my drive to see light spill out of the window
onto my lawn and forget, for a moment
in that welcome, who could possibly be there.

Robert Kroetsch

The Cow in the Quicksand and How I(t) Got Out
Responding to Stegner's Wolf Willow

I came to these prairies twice. One time I was born here; one time I arrived as an adult. I was born in Alberta in 1927; I arrived in Winnipeg from Upstate New York in an aging green four-door Dodge Dart in 1978. By that duplicity I might have wished to gain a surplus of perception. Accidentally, I inherited two deaths.

Design and accident combine in our writing of this landlocked and skylocked terrain. Just fly from Winnipeg to Regina or to St. Paul, watch the mapped land and the movement of clouds.

When I was a boy drinking Orange Crush in the Canada Cafe in Heisler, Alberta, the farmers who had eaten dinner (the noon meal) sometimes offered to flip a coin and to pay Wong Toy either double or nothing. What I remember is the terror and elation I, a listening boy, felt at the speaking of that wager. I remember neither the winners nor the losers.

Double or nothing somehow became the wager by which I might live a prairie life. I recognized even then how hard farmers—and also the chinaman, as we called him—worked for a living. They did not work for money, they worked for a living. That too was a lesson. And I marveled at the mystery of their working so hard by design and then risking so much to chance.

They wore the weather close to their skin, those prairie people. Rain and drought and hail and snow—the varieties of weather had a way of riding out of the farther west on the same horse. "Double or nothing," the farmers said. I liked the way the coin leapt off the flicked thumb, spun high in the ferocious light, hesitated. You had to make your call while the coin was still in the air.

A careful misreading is one of my rules; it makes for creative errors. I was a writer for a long time before Dennis Cooley wrote "Fielding," and yet when I read that text I recognized in it a prior text that had enabled me to write. Time is another peevish mystery on these Great Central Plains. I quote at length from Cooley:

i remember you
years later in the white light
bent on our 55 Massey
dragging the rusted discer
over Evendon's section 7 miles north of town
its steel plates glinting on the rub of dirt
and the loud sudden scrape of rocks
grinding off sparks
your striped engineer's cap ruling the redness
in a clean line across your forehead
(the startling white softness of your body
underneath the gray cotton shirt you always wore)
and the sweet smell of the soap and cream
you pulled through the zipper of
your pebble-grained leather shaving kit
on Saturday nights and how in good spirits
we rolled down the gravel road
over the big hill under
the orange slant of the sun
with Hank Snow blowing us down into Estevan
from CHAB in Moose Jaw yellow
on the radio of our '53 green Ford
    Just to think it could be
    Time has opened the door
    And at last I am free
    I don't hurt anymore

and how the new mercury vapour street lights
would take us in their blueness past
the dazzling forkclinks and the lemonhalibut smells
fanning from the Canada Cafe
direct to the onoffonoffon incandescence drawing us
dreaming into the deep violet shade of the Orpheum theatre
where for 15 cents we witnessed
Gene Autry "the singing cowboy"
rescuing forlorn women in flickering melodrama.

"I remember you," Cooley begins this section of his poem
for and about his father, and in the blur of pronouns we let
ourselves or we welcome ourselves into the poem—or we are
seduced into its small and overwhelming journey, and time
disintegrates softly.

His Canada Cafe was mine; I know that for sure. His. Mine. I.
. . . We are in that landscape and from it; we share a climate, a
history, a set of conditions social and cultural and economic that
carry us into a narrative of Saturday night in a prairie town.

Or is it a narrative of how place is turned into poem? Or is it,
to be more reckless, a narrative of the father, the lost father, himself
rescued in the guise of forlorn women? And why do we flinch
with pleasure, hearing those lines in parentheses: "(the startling
white softness of your body / underneath the gray cotton shirt
you always wore)"? And what is the connection between that
figure at work in the fields and the trip "into the deep violet shade
of the Orpheum theatre"? And who among us dares the singer's
task? Or the singer's journey to the land of the dead?

To be a writer one must be, whatever else, a reader. One
recognizes in texts the doubles that allow the writing self into the
recognitions that become words.

I'm going to proceed by responding to a book that I in a sense
read before it was written, then read again after it was written.
That is one of the advantages of bargaining oneself into a maze
of wins and losses. "Matching," we called it, strangely, there in
the Canada Cafe. *Matching* to see who would win, who lose. And
of course one hopes that Orpheus will make the attempt once

more to rescue the dead bride—even if one is oneself, like Cooley's "Fielding," that missing person.

Or to reverse the coin—perhaps the gaze is all we have that is special to us, as writers in this landscape. Language comes after; language is an announcement of deathly consequence. To begin to write is, already, to accept loss.

The 49th Parallel is a line. A line of writing. That bizarre name suggests at once an abundance and an absurdity. Like most names, in its very claim to exactness it wins enormous power. The Medicine Line, the Sioux said. Don't cross that line, we say, desiring at once safety and transgression. Or: I'm going across the line today, we say in Winnipeg, to shop for cheap booze in Grand Forks.

By a paradox that inscribes and erases that line, a quintessentially Canadian text was written by a quintessentially American writer. In 1955, Wallace Stegner published a book called *Wolf Willow: A History, A Story, and a Memory of the Last Plains Frontier*.

The subtitle announces our temptations. We are tempted to write a history, with all its claims to authenticity, to validation by research, to generalizations that assert themselves as truths. But against all that we know—as lovers know each other—the temptation to tell a story. We know the impulse to exaggerate the ramifications and the delight, to leave out where leaving out speeds up the plot, to clarify the hero by a reckless but admirable spending, to separate good from bad by summary execution.

A memory, Stegner says. Against both history and fabulation, against both the supposed exactness of history and the artifice of story—not a memoir, but a *memory*. Against those larger and intimidating designs looms here, in our landscape, the astounded and the astounding voice of self (and I invite you: read Tom McGrath, read Lorna Crozier, read David Arnason or Dave Williamson or Patrick Friesen or Jan Horner or Di Brandt); we as readers listen, and in our listening we hear the prairie/plains strategy that pretends against all pretension in its simple claim: but I was there.

Stegner wrote his book out of a long absence and a brief return. Born in 1908, he was a child on his parents' homestead in southwest Saskatchewan from 1914 to 1920; writing of that place as a "middle-aged pilgrim" he could say: "Our homestead lay . . . right on the Saskatchewan-Montana border—a place so ambiguous in its affiliations that we felt as uncertain as the drainage about which way to flow."

Ambiguity, Stegner cautions us, "gazing" from a distance, standing close, is one of his themes. Sometimes to name is to possess; sometimes a dictionary is the catalog of our hesitations.

When I was a boy, living in the parklands and not on the true prairies at all, we children in spring used to strip the outer bark off a branch of silver willow and chew the sweet, stringy inner bark and believe that winter was over. The taste of the bark of that willow—silver willow, wolf willow—says to me what the smell of its leaves said to Stegner: this is the various place we call home.

Stegner offers a huge and difficult generalization about us prairie dwellers. He begins his book by talking about "the drama of this landscape" and he goes on to say, "It is a country to breed mystical people, egocentric people, perhaps poetic people."

It is no accident, and a happy accident too, that Stegner makes us uneasy with his use of the verb, to breed.

By design or accident, we have found in the image of the horse the dramatic juncture of sky and earth; in novels as widely different in content and intention as Sinclair Ross's *As For Me and My House* and Sharon Butala's *The Gates of the Sun*, the horse figures our predicament—and reminds us that the novel had its beginning in another landlocked and open landscape. Cervantes, in the country that apparently gave the horse to our landscape, gave us the story of Don Quixote, his feet not quite on the ground, his head not quite in the sky.

"It is a country to breed mystical people. . . ." And while I am not quite sure I know what mystical is, I have a suspicion I believe what Stegner says.

Mysticism, as I feel the word in my bones, has something to do with whatever it is that can't be fully articulated. As a prairie writer I've committed myself to speaking the unspeakable, and unspeakable here is a pun. My Aunt Mary told me not to say what I was saying. My critics ask me what it is I'm trying to say.

I'm talking about our very unwillingness as well as our inability to speak the name of all that we are. I'm reminded of the claim that, during the Dirty Thirties, farmers stopped naming their farms—because the names made the farms too easy for money collectors to find.

Our strategies, even when we claim to tell the God's own truth, are strategies of evasion. We are so often trying to slip out of the grip of someone or something. I won't attempt to name that someone or something, but in the metonymic slithering of the world it might appear briefly as a tornado, more enduringly as a political leader.

We who are from Minnesota and the Dakotas, from Saskatchewan and Manitoba, share not only a set of borders but also a variety of temptations, of alibis, of curses placed upon our minds and bodies, of outrageous joys, of furtive pleasures. I'm not attempting here an examination of place. I'm asking how the plains or the prairies enable us to recognize ourselves as writers, then enable us to write.

I should caution the reader that I'm renowned for my ability to misread the question—even my own—and for my ability to answer the question by indirection, misdirection, deferral, delay, rhetorical dodges, postmodern artifice, sexual innuendo, and just plain outright lies.

I find it fascinating that even so realistic a novelist as Sharon Butala, a hardboiled rancher from Stegner's own "last plains frontier," sees in our landscape and in the drama of that landscape the figure of Coyote. Perhaps to be mystical, in our world, is to have doings with the trickster.

But then, consider the opening of Butala's *The Gates of the Sun*, published thirty years after the appearance of *Wolf Willow*. This is from the first opening, the opening lines in italics that is a dream and contradicts its dreaming:

> *He remembered a river, wide, flat, silver. It went on forever in every direction and far off from where he stood. People in miniature boats bobbed on its surface, without purpose or direction, like leaves on a puddle. Or rose and*

floated in the sky, above the water's surface, on a silver
streak. Had he dreamt it, perhaps? No, somehow they had
crossed a river and he had clung to his mother's black-
gloved hand.

And three paragraphs later:

The journey, as time went on, tumbled out of a
confusion of sensations to a series of clear and bright, but
disconnected pictures: the long, jolting ride on the hard
wooden wagonseat, the instant when his mother's hands
were larger and reddened in the sun, the horses' flanks
tightening and releasing. And the green of the Cypress
Hills.

I'm willing to call this mysticism, this description of arrival, once
more from across the line, in the green of Stegner's Cypress Hills.

There is so often something apocryphal about our stories. They
are secret stories. They stand outside our own canonical notion
of what the story should be. They are, in ontological ways, of
doubtful authorship.

In a prairie/plains world that insists by daylight that we are
perfectly sensible people, the stories come as mysteriously as
the horses to young Andrew Samson in the second opening of
The Gates of the Sun. In that opening he is awakened from dream
by a sound. He steps outside the shack in which he lives with
his mother:

The full moon struck him, froze him in its white light.
. . . They came into view. An endless herd, flowing past,
through the unfenced, undefined yard, an immense herd
of horses split in their flow by the house, the barn, the
corral, so that they were in front of him and behind him,
approaching on one hand and leaving on the other.

Butala gives us those two matched and at the same time
different openings. The flow. The dream become reality, the
reality become dream. The definition and the resistance to

definition. Cooley's father's Orpheum. The mysticism. We are of two minds.

More recklessly and dangerously, Stegner suggests this is a country to breed egocentric people.

In what sense egocentric? We writers pride ourselves on our sense of the tribal. Margaret Laurence, Mark Vinz, Rudy Wiebe, Aritha van Herk, Bart Schneider, Sandra Birdsell, are only a few of the names that come to mind. We dream of knowing the extravagances of tribal union implicit in Robert Bly's *Sleepers Joining Hands.*

But *egotistical,* Stegner insists. And perhaps he means that in the absence of traditional culture and its elaborated implications we fall back on our own experience. Stegner writes: "However anachronistic I may be, I am a product of the American earth, and in nothing quite so much as in the contrast between what I knew through the pores and what I was officially taught."

When I read those lines, at the University of Iowa, in the home state of Stegner's mother—when I read those lines I knew I was reading the credo of my own discontent. I was at the time a graduate student, studying the tradition that I had somehow to learn to appreciate; and I was learning from Stegner that I had to learn, in the process of accepting the tradition, how to resist it. I knew that I too, Canadian, was a product of the American earth, and there in those square and sensible buildings, on the banks of a small river, surrounded by beautiful fields of corn, inhaling the air that all summer long stank to high heaven of pig shit—and to this day I stir to that smell, thinking wild thoughts of Transcendentalism—there, I began to understand the saving grace of, and the insistent need for, the egotistical.

Let me tell you a story.

And by the way, Stegner is exact to the point of definitiveness when he says, "You grow up speaking one dialect and reading and writing another." And of course that is at the heart of the problem and that is part of the reason why this country breeds "perhaps a poetic people." In writers as different as William Gass and Eli Mandel, in writers as close and as far apart as Meridel Le Sueur and Carol Shields and Carol Bly, we see the eruption of words into the gap between the two dialects that contain and open up our lives.

But I was going to tell you a story, and perhaps I am telling you a story. Between the years when Wallace Stegner was a child on the Frenchman River and the time when he published his book, I as a child paid a visit to what at the time we called the Whitemud River. But come to think of it, that's what Stegner resolved to call it.

My visit took place during my first time on the prairies, before I went away and read *Wolf Willow* and came back. The chronology of a story is either difficult or a lie, I find.

I grew up two hundred miles north of the American border, in what is called Central Alberta. The town of Eastend, Saskatchewan sits on the banks of the Whitemud, just a few miles north of the line. I had an aunt, Aunt Maggie, in nearby Shaunavon; she was married to a homesteader from St. Paul who hadn't laid eyes on a farm until he found himself farming. My father had homesteaded for two years just north of Shaunavon, before homesickness drove him to join most of his Ontario family where it was homesteading in Alberta. He had friends in Eastend.

In 1936 my father bought a new green four-door Ford. I remember vividly because when we went to pick up the car I was teased about the car dealer's daughter, Belva Jacobs, and as a result I fiddled with the handle of the door on the drive home and accidentally opened the door and accidentally fell out of the car. An early experience of falling in love and one that continues to inform my prairie life.

But I was going to tell you a story.

My father, having bought the car, revealed he had bought it because we were about to embark on what could only be described as an epic journey—to visit relatives and friends in southern Saskatchewan.

I remember our first encounter with abandoned farms. Our first look at dried-out country. I remember my father stopping the car in what seemed the open middle of nowhere; he and my mother and we three kids got out of the car to stare in disbelief at the bare fields that should have been fields of wheat. I remember the hammer and blur of grasshoppers on the flat windshield. I remember our first encounter with playmates who stopped playing and ran behind a granary to vomit, because of what they were or weren't eating.

I was nine years old. When we got to Eastend, I was convinced we had come to the end of something; to this day the name, Eastend, fills me with images of falling off the edge of the world. That too is in the nature of love.

We were visiting people who lived in a house near the Whitemud River. It was in that house I first heard about the cow in the quicksand.

For much of a lifetime now, two narrative possibilities—two speech acts—have quarreled in my mind.

Part of me is persuaded that I actually saw the cow in the quicksand. That part of me is still horrified at the sight of the cow, its head and the thin line of its backbone showing in the quicksand, the terrified cow snorting, frothing at the mouth, the helpless men trying to get a lariat onto a cow's head without themselves getting stuck, then succeeding, then discovering that by tying the lariat to the bumper of a car high up on the riverbank they would only succeed in dismembering or even beheading the cow.

There is another part of me that suggests I never actually saw the cow. That part of me suggests that I and the other kids were told the story to keep us from playing along the riverbanks and down in the drying quicksand and risking our lives.

In that version the horror is of a different and possibly more ominous nature.

We were told the quicksand had no bottom. We have on the prairies various notions of bottomless, some of them having to do with going to hell. I remember that the Battle River was said to have no bottom, and when one of my uncles took me fishing there I sat motionless in the middle of the old rowboat, not yet knowing I was by accident to acquire a surplus of deaths. When one of the Messner boys dived into Dried Meat Lake and didn't surface, ever, people said it was no wonder the searchers couldn't find young Glen, he had dived in a place where the lake had no bottom.

I liked those stories. They became part of a novel I wrote years ago, *The Words of My Roaring*. But the business with the quicksand was different—still is different. When I began to realize that of all the stories that surround us, only a few take hold of our minds and shape our lives—by the time I got to that realization, it was too late to decide between the two versions of what happened.

My only justification for making a private difficulty public is a hard-earned suspicion that here on the plains/prairies, just as we often talk between two dialects, so must we often talk between two versions of the story. It is no accident that Wallace Stegner, the writer who rode away in order to write, returning to the town he calls Whitemud, encounters most painfully, most tellingly, the writer figure, Corky Jones—the double who did not leave at all, who could never leave.

I return to Dennis Cooley and his poem for and about his father and the quote from Hank Snow:

Just to think it could be
Time has opened the door
And at least I am free
I don't hurt anymore

But, theory and hope alike be damned, the fact remains, the cow is in the quicksand.

Surely one of the intentions of literature is just this: to acquaint us with the dangers of and to coax us into intimacies with the landscapes we wear. I remember a tailor in England who was fitting me for a suit; he checked my fly and asked in a voice at once elegant and discreet, "Sir, do you dress to the left or to the right?"—a question that to this day makes me slip unobtrusively into men's stores, or women's stores for that matter, and hesitate insanely in front of full-length mirrors.

"You grow up speaking one dialect and reading and writing another." Stegner's book locates his dictum in story-telling itself. We feel the gap between the stories we know in our pores—the stories we feel in the daily weather of our lives—and the stories we are officially taught.

But how do the plains enable us to recognize ourselves as writers, then enable us to write? Stegner insinuates an explanation:

> . . . I have not forgotten the licking I got when, aged about six, I was caught playing with my father's loaded .30-.30 that hung above the mantel just under the Rosa Bonheur painting of three white horses in a storm. After that licking I lay out behind the chopping block all one afternoon watching my big dark father as he worked at one thing and another, and all the time I lay there I kept aiming an empty cartridge case at him and dreaming murder.

That dream of murder—that possibly impotent dream of murder—Stegner tells us in the next paragraph, remembering vividly, has faded. "My mother too," he goes on, "who saved me from him so many times, and once missed saving me when he clouted me with a chunk of stove wood and knocked me·over the woodbox and broke my collarbone: she too has faded." Except that the book bears a dedication: "This is in memory of my mother."

Stegner would escape the flipped coin that won't declare itself by claiming the death of history, the survival however ambiguously of memory. But, having declared that allegiance, he plunders historical documents for the making of much of his book.

Resisting history, we take on the burden of a concealed history. Claiming to remember, we discover the slippage that transforms memory into history and fiction alike.

I've announced in my title that the cow gets out of the quicksand. I'm sweating. Remembering Dennis Cooley's poem and its reference in parentheses to "the startling white softness of your body," I'm reminded of my own father.

My father's skin, from his sunburnt neck down, was almost grotesquely the skin of a boy, even when he was my present age. That was because he, a farmer and a rancher for fifty years, never once when out of doors took off his shirt or so much as rolled up his shirt sleeves. He had that kind of abiding respect for the prairie sun.

I offer this curious detail as evidence of his careful relationship to the truths of the world he lived in. He ran cattle in the valley of the Battle River; he grew wheat and oats and barley on the flat land above the valley. And, yes, he told stories.

He was a considerable story-teller. But he claimed no interest in fiction; he trusted rather to the accuracies of his own memory. And that was the power he had over us. I always meant to ask him about the cow in the quicksand, and I dearly regret now that I didn't. But my not asking was the only power I had. It was the only way I had of aiming the cartridge case.

And if the story of the cow was told to us kids—was used against us, one might say—not to elaborate our sense of the world, not to give us a sense of freedom and responsibility, but rather to manipulate us—then we had a right and even an obligation to appropriate the story, with all its errors of intention and detail, and make an effort to tell what was not told.

The margin speaks its one small chance against the design of the center, and on that speaking everything turns.

It was getting on in the afternoon when the adults told us the story; they wanted to be rid of minding kids and get on with having a beer.

In a marvelous passage in *Wolf Willow* Stegner allows:

> As the prairie taught me identity by exposing me, the river valley taught me about safety. In a jumpy and insecure childhood where all masculine elements are painful or dangerous, sanctuary matters. That sunken bottom sheltered from the total sky and the untrammeled wind was my hibernating ground, my place of snugness, and in a country often blistered and crisped, green became the color of safety. When I feel the need to return to the womb, this is still the place toward which my well-conditioned unconscious turns like an old horse heading for the barn.

There were four or five boys, two or three girls, in our group. We were a gang, and I suppose hard to manage. Families were bigger in those days. My oldest sister, briefly younger than I, was not with us; she has a ferocious memory for detail and tends to blister every account I give of our childhood. Pat would not go with us; she was on the side of history and law even then. But the rest of us, warned about the cow, dodged around behind the house, past my dad's new Ford, and headed straight for the river.

And sure enough, would you believe it: there was a cow in the quicksand.

We kids had to work fast. We had to wrestle and drag two or three huge planks that we weren't quite big enough to carry; we had to scare up a lariat; we had to find a shovel.

Stegner is right. How explain the unconscious, out on the bald prairie? Where do you find the womb? Sharon Butala tells that terrifying story about young Andrew cutting the dead calf out of the cow.

We kids went through the wolf willow, down over the clay banks where mud swallows nested, onto the treacherous sand. Out of the wind, down there, the smell of dead fish and dead animals was sweet and somehow inviting on the air. We laid two planks end to end, there at the edge of the drying river that was more slough than river that summer day.

We called the cow Bossy. We didn't know her name, but we talked to her, somehow. We talked to the cow. That calmed her down. Then we felt calmer too; we got the lariat onto her neck. We didn't want to strangle the cow, pulling. One of the boys tried to make a halter, but he didn't quite know how. One of the girls said we should get a rope onto the cow's front legs. We knelt on a plank and dug with the shovel and our bare hands and got the cow's right foreleg free enough so someone could, at great personal risk, reach down and get the lariat around the upper part of the leg.

I've done research on quicksand; it's the shape of the grain of sand that causes all the trouble; the grains are round, like ballbearings; instead of packing down they give way, yield to a weight placed upon them. On top of all that, when you pull up you create a kind of vacuum under the object you're trying to free from the sand.

We pulled and hoisted for a long time before Bossy came free. But all of a sudden, just like that, she was up to where she could help us, she had her front legs on the plank we were trying to slide beneath her.

She was a three-titter, that cow. This may seem a strange detail, but to us kids, who had grown up on the prairies, it said something. A lot of milkcows, those days, got at least one tit frozen or caught in barbed wire. We never said teat those days, we said tit; teat was a word I learned years later, from an embarrassed teacher; again, a problem in naming and in the relation of education to this our earth, and these the pores of our bodies. That cow had suffered enough, it didn't need any more suffering.

We realized, we kids, we had the detail that would cinch our story. We had won. We had *matched* the adults. When we went up out of the valley of the Whitemud and back to where the adults were having their beer, and when we told them, there really was a cow in the quicksand, you know, and you must know which one—that good milker, the three-titter—then they would have to believe our story.

They would have to regret they lied to us in the first place.

Books referred to:

Butala, Sharon. *The Gates of the Sun.* Saskatoon: Fifth House, 1985.

Cooley, Dennis. *Leaving.* Winnipeg: Turnstone Press, 1980.

Stegner, Wallace. *Wolf Willow: A History, a Story, and a Memory of the Last Plains Frontier.* New York: The Viking Press, Viking Compass Edition, 1967 (1955).

Jay Meek

Surprising Nights

There's no doubt that my life surprises me,
like a handgun stuffed in a toiletries bag,

but even sleeping outdoors under the stars
can be claustrophobic, like a planetarium.

This afternoon, when I recited the planets
following one another around the far turn,

I saw the motorcycles I once looked down on
as a child with my uncle at the cyclorama.

It was fantastic. We just stood on the rim
while the fierce men whirled on their bikes

around and around as they rode those walls
under the big sky, under its small glitter.

Walking the Mall

In winter, before the shops open,
we walk the mall for exercise,
going two by two, sometimes waving
as if we were all neighbors
who felt safe with one another.
Shopping malls are grand places
and early morning in winter
they're mysterious, with all of us
making the rounds as if we had
some place to get to, like snowbirds
already gone to Florida.

        At West Acres in Fargo,
there's a glass display case
called the Roger Maris Museum.
It's like a long window
to a sport shop without doors,
and inside is the home run ball
he hit off Jack Fisher.
It holds a lot to think about,
like the spring morning
I stood over his grave
with two friends who are good poets.

Where the old ball park used to be
maybe there's a fire station,
or a stand of pines in the outfield
where Roger Maris played
in the Pioneer League his first year.
That's what happened to the park
in Grand Forks, where he hit one out,
and whenever I drive past now

I imagine fans leaving the stands
after the cheering is done
and driving around town for years,
until one winter morning
they somehow pull into the mall
to walk up and down,
just for good memories and the sport.

North from Deadwood

I'm driving home through our national grasslands,
the light long over the range,
and when I pull my rental car into a lookout park
carved into one end of a butte,
a few sheep start to cross in front of me,
not very efficiently, but somehow they get across
with only a little bleating,
while the grasses go on bending down and waving.

Back on the road, I see some mule deer racing me
out across the valley,
and I am struck by the insistence
of everything that lives, that replenishes itself.
If I ever had a love of cars, I renounce it,
and the culture of cars.
I renounce Charlotte and Indianapolis and Daytona.
What could I have imagined as a boy
when I drove tanks and jeeps through the white sand?

I renounce all tanks and antitank missile launchers.
Steering nobs and raccoon tails.
I drive up along the badlands, turn at Watford City,
the day pretty well toward being over
for this part of the world.
Once, I pass a Lutheran church out on the prairie,
its front door blown out,
the steeple stacked up beside it.
It reminds me of a man
standing beside his baseball cap on the sidewalk,
just standing there and weeping.

Postcard from the Center of the Continent
Rugby, North Dakota

The big story from out here
is that on the face
of things, the Center Motel
stands just a little

off-center, given the cairn
across the road
that marks the true center,
there by the diner

where a newspaper dispenser
holds all the clarities
a tired body cares to know,
and wants a rest from.

Even the cement block walls
pictured on the card
show what whitewash means
in towns like this,

and in the emptiness of sky
I weigh the lasting creed
of Lutheran churches
deserted now on the prairie.

How plain everything looks
here at the center,
except for those ornaments
the size of globes

rising over the motel facade
from a decade of cars
with great fins,
all those stalled years

when everybody believed
that if you kept up
a good appearance
you could go almost anywhere.

Friends and Neighbors Day

Standing in the shadow of a hangar
at the Grand Forks Air Base,
I look in the cockpits
of fighters, the F-11 and F-14,

then walk the ramp of a transport.
Inside, it's as deserted
as the rib cage of a brontosaurus.
Under the wing of a DC-3

the Canadian Air Force flew in,
a family of Hutterites
passes by with its own version
of peace. If I have one,

I know it doesn't easily include
anything like rail garrisons
or the thousand silos
we've drilled in our wheatfields

to hang missiles in suspension,
while we pipe in fresh air
at a temperature
a successful farmer would drive

as far as Ft. Lauderdale to find.
At each installation
and wing, there's an enlisted man
saying what the job is

he hopes he'll never have to do.
Everybody's friendly today,
and in the hangar bay
there's a dance band of farmers

playing tunes as old as the DC-3.
The smell of roast buffalo
rises from the grill
near planes where precision pilots,

the Blue Angels, work a hot crowd,
lifting infants in their arms
and signing autographs
as if they were stars of the show.

Cries

Waking in my motel room,
I turn on the television
to hear some human voice,
words to sound the day

we rise to. Nothing's on
only a newscaster made up
to glamorize the horrors
we can't put out of mind.

Last night, I woke to hear
one wall shaking, the bed
in the next room slamming
up against it, love cries

rising until they burst.
Last week, another motel;
the same cries all night.
Whichever way I turned,

I dreamed in the next room
a woman was being stripped
of her skin, long strands
peeled away as she watched

it happen, intense pain
broken only by the absence
of pain. If I dreamed it,
whose cries did I wake to?

I listened at the near wall:
no male sound, no sweetness.
I thought of burn victims
who are suspended in water,

the anguish of cool wards
after sudden explosions—
nights of petroleum fires
burning on through morning.

Perhaps during the night
the lovers heard me cry
from some solitary depth
beyond their own diving,

until rising from our beds
we stood at the one wall,
our faces pressed so close
that we could have kissed.

Out

Out here, the nights
are long all winter,
and nothing thaws.

I suppose it's about
the same all over.
One day a man came

to give a workshop
on grief, a rabbi
from Boston, or

a suburb of Boston,
and hundreds
of folks who went

came away weeping,
carrying his books
under their arms.

He must go to town
after town, maybe
thousands of places

where grief touches
someone just waking,
or shining shoes.

I suppose it's good
that somebody comes
to say it's all right

if we want to weep,
it's only human
to want a little more

from life, when people
don't know what to
make of their lives,

except that they wear,
hang loosely on them,
and ache to break out.

In Charge of Laughter

In the old television situation comedies,
somebody had to put in the laughter for days
when the audience sat on their hands,
ready to leave. But it didn't occur to us

that an actual person finally had to decide
not only what was funny, but which comic
got the best laughs, and that we were relieved
simultaneously of the burden of choice

and of laughter. Maybe here was a person
who tried to raise us out of ourselves,
or just someone good at making us break out
in wave after wave of cruel laughter.

We might have said it was like being saved.
For what we were given was the effect
and not the cause, or maybe some consequence
in excess of any cause, both pointed

and arbitrary, like the compliments a host
receives after the guests have gone home,
doubled over from something
agreed upon as having been devastating.

Kathleen Norris

The Sky Is Full of Blue & Full of the Mind of God

A girl wrote that once
for me, in winter, in a school
at the Minot Air Force Base.
A girl tall for her age,
with cornrows and a shy, gap-toothed smile.
She was lonely in North Dakota,
I think: for God, for trees,
warm weather, the soft cadences of Louisiana.
I think of her as the sky stretches tight
all around.

I'm at the Conoco on I-94, waiting for the eastbound bus.
Mass is not over: the towers of the monastery
give no sign that, deep in the church,
men in robes and chasubles
are playing at a serious game.

I feel like dancing on this
wooden porch: "Gotta get to you, baby,
been runnin' all over town."
The jukebox is wired to be heard outside
and I dance to keep warm,
my breath carried white on the breeze.

The sky stretches tight, a mandorla of cloud
around the sun. And now
Roy Orbison reaches for the stratosphere:
something about a blue angel.
It is the Sanctus; I know it; I'm ready.

Dakota: Or, Gambling, Garbage, and the New Ghost Dance

The Dakotas are America's Empty Quarter, with the population of Manhattan, about a million and a half people, spread over an area three times larger than New York State. Few appreciate the harsh beauty of a land that rolls like the ocean floor it once was, where dry winds scour out buttes, and the temperature can reach 110 degrees above or plunge to thirty below for a week or more. Say what you will about our climate, in Dakota we say it "keeps the riffraff out."

But Dakota bravado masks an anxiety that afflicts forgotten people in a mass-market society. We boast about our isolation, and the lengths we go to to overcome it; I like to tell about the time I drove four hundred miles round trip to hear William Stafford read his poetry. We laugh when Bismarck, South Dakota is mentioned on the national news. We shrug when North and South Dakota are routinely omitted from magazine advertisements for "national" stores and services. And we learn not to be surprised when the Environmental Protection Agency reports that big cities back east want to dump their garbage in our "wide open spaces." Given the dismal state of our economy, some Dakota towns are clamoring for the dollars the garbage industry would bring.

It's not inspiring to have the Black Hills, the sacred Paha Sapa of the Sioux, classified as a "world-class site" by waste disposal companies, or to have the military move bomb-scoring sites onto our ranches. The Air Force uses the Dakotas to practice for Siberia;

low-flying bombers from the air bases at Rapid City, Minot and Grand Forks are a common sight on our prairie. My initiation came on a farm one day with a burst of noise and a huge plane flying over so low I could see the human form in the cockpit. "B-52," said the farmer, laconically. Now the planes are sleek B-1s. The Plains also harbor many of the country's nuclear missiles. Several silos are situated less than five miles from a town. Dakotans tend to support a strong national defense, and we've paid for it by being placed at ground zero.

I've begun thinking of the Dakotas as "the new Old South," an image that was reinforced not long ago when South Dakota dropped to fiftieth place among the states in average teacher salary, a position that had been held by Mississippi for years. We've also begun to surpass the South in harboring the poorest counties in the nation. The Dakotas are now attracting industry in much the way the Old South did, by offering low taxes and reliable, semi-skilled workers who are used to living in a minimum-wage economy. A 1983 article in *Forbes* on South Dakota's pursuit of out-of-state businesses was called "Let's Make a Deal." Mostly overlooked in all this is the fact that we're in danger of becoming what a friend has termed "Taiwan on the Prairie."

There are even uncanny echoes of the Old South in the literary world, where it's always been more acceptable to be from the South than from South Dakota. In the 1980s books set in the Dakotas began to receive mention in *The New York Times Book Review*. But the price of this acceptance may prove high. It's the mythologized Old South that's acceptable to readers outside the region, and I fear that the same will be true for Dakota. We could face a situation like the Native Americans of one hundred years ago who, as their culture was being destroyed, came to be seen as romantic. Indian children were punished for speaking their own language, but Indian words were taken and used to sell a myth of freedom on the American road. Pontiac, Cherokee, even the sacred Thunderbird.

In the mid-1980s a "Dakota chic" surfaced in America, both in stylish restaurants in New York City and in national advertising campaigns. Dakota Beer came onto the market with ads focused on "wheat from the heartland and the people who grow it." The ads were filmed in Montana, but as one South Dakota official put it, with typical effacement, "at least they came to within a state of us." The Chrysler Corporation flew real Dakota cowboys and Indians to Hollywood to pose in their new Dakota pickup trucks. It's ironic that in the year the beer came out, over twenty percent of South Dakota's farmers, the good folk growing that wheat, either left or seriously contemplated leaving their land for economic reasons, and so many auto and farm implement dealers closed that people might have had to drive a hundred miles or more to buy the truck, if they could afford it. That year, in the 576 Zip Code area where I live, the median per capita income was $8200.

Western Dakota is remarkably isolated, both physically and psychologically, and a sense of loss haunts many whose immigrant families prospered after World War II, as they, or their children, became a new underclass, farmers on food stamps. The isolation affects the poor in particularly severe ways. People who are laid off in my town have to travel a hundred miles to a Job Service office in order to get their benefits; there is no public transportation on the route. Physical isolation, all but forgotten in this age of supersonic jets, is real enough if you have to travel, as I do, 125 miles to an airport.

Ironically, the Dakotas were less isolated fifty years ago, when passenger trains stopped in every little town. In the 1930s my mother could take the train from Lemmon, South Dakota, to college in Chicago, and for a time in the late 1950s United Airlines had scheduled flights in and out of Lemmon. The town had a population of 3500 then. We're down to 1700 today, and the nearest public transportation is a Greyhound flag stop at a gas station eighty miles north. If I'm going south, east or west, the distance is two hundred miles or more. Many communities now offer, with government assistance, limited public transportation to senior citizens visiting regional medical centers. But deregulation during the 1980s made travel here much more expensive and difficult.

With small towns shrinking and services eroding, many Dakotans retain an appalling innocence as to what it means to be rural in contemporary America. The year we lost our Penney's store, young people were quoted in the town's weekly newspaper as saying they'd like to see a McDonald's or a K-Mart open up. They have not been taught one basic of modern American capitalism: the market is everything. Since there is no market here, nothing that counts demographically, it's as if we don't exist.

Our invisibility to the rest of America, our lack of the numbers that would allow us more voice in influencing either big business or big corporations, is turning all Dakotans into an underclass. Native Americans are still the most poor and invisible among us; but now that the vast majority of our people live in the eastern half of the Dakotas, western Dakotans are increasingly invisible to more affluent eastern Dakotans; Dakotans as a whole are invisible to the rest of America.

In self-defense, rural Dakotans have become more insular, more isolated in spirit. In my town, it's become unusual for young people to venture outside the region to go to school, yet most parents know that they must raise their children for the world outside. There are few job opportunities here.

Increasingly on the Plains we are becoming victims of our own mythology. As our towns are failing and our lives here become less viable, many Dakotans cling stubbornly to a myth of independence. In fact, the Dakotas have always been more or less a colony in America, remarkably dependent on outside interests. I feel it every time I sell wheat for less than it costs to produce, or when I have to sell my grass-fed cattle to be fattened and pumped full of chemicals in a feed-lot.

In recent years even the idol of "local control" that so appeals to our sense of ourselves as independent frontier types has been used against us. When First Bank Systems pulled out of our town a few years ago, the article in the town paper spoke in glowing terms about how wonderful it was that local people were going to have the chance to invest in their own bank. In the Minneapolis papers the move out of small towns was described as one that would enable First Bank to provide more "sophisticated consumer services" to urban and suburban Minnesotans. *The Wall Street Journal* told the whole truth: the move dropping all the bad agricultural loans was applauded as good business, and First Bank stock soared.

Many colonial economies are based on tourism, and the Dakotas have begun to pursue that aggressively, often offering gambling as a lure. But this, along with our fledgling waste industry, is not particularly good for our self-esteem. Nor does it alter the traditional "boom and bust" economy of the region. And there's always the danger that in selling ourselves to tourists, we may destroy what drew us, and them, to the area in the first place.

People do know why they like living here. For one thing, life is still lived on a human scale. When I lived in New York City in the early 1970s I found that I could not cash a check at another branch of my bank, no matter how much identification I showed. What a luxury to find, on moving to South Dakota, that I could write a counter-check (a blank check on which I write in my own account number) at towns within a hundred-mile radius, without showing any identification at all. It may be odd to think of life in Dakota as a luxury, but beyond the trust that this sort of transaction implies, it is the sort of service that makes life easier, that is offered to the wealthy at a price, say the cost of an American Express Gold Card. The irony of Dakota "luxury" is that only the poor may be able to afford it.

One of the simple pleasures of the poor is driving where there's no traffic to speak of. One moonlit night I traveled the two hundred miles from Rapid City to home and saw fewer than twenty other vehicles and more than one hundred antelope. Most days I take a long walk at dawn, and sometimes I'm greeted with a spectacular moonset, a huge globe as orange as a harvest moon. There's usually no sound to speak of, except for wind and the occasional truck on the highway a mile away. Just me and earth and sky.

In western Dakota I've walked through miniature Grand Canyons few humans have ever seen, through sweeps of land that put John Ford vistas, and even the scenery in *Dances with Wolves*, to shame. Our odd, rolling landscape terrifies many people; some think it's as barren as the moon. But others are possessed by it. "The land lives," is how one young rancher put it to me. But I fear that his attitude will prove as incomprehensible to modern, urban Americans as a similar reverence for the land among Native Americans did to the white settlers of a century ago.

In 1974, when I was asked to write an essay about my move from New York City to Lemmon, South Dakota, I spoke of being haunted by "the sense that we are all Indians here, as much in danger of losing our land as the Indians of one hundred years ago. And, if it happens, I fear we will meet with the same massive national indifference." I do not wish to minimize the particular sufferings that have been and continue to be inflicted on Native Americans, but the "farm crisis" of the 1980s leads me to believe I was on to something. And others have made the connection. I once heard a Lakota holy man say to college students at the University of North Dakota, "Farmers are the next Indians, going through the same thing we did." The students were fairly rude to him, not listening. He was just an old man, just an Indian. But when he asked, "How many of us are going to stand beside the farmers and see justice done for these people?" there was finally silence in the room. At least a few of the students, the ones from farms, had wondered that themselves.

In the Ghost Dance religion of just a hundred years ago, a desperate people turned to their ancestors for help against the white soldiers and settlers. Lakota warriors wore shirts they believed the white soldiers' bullets could not penetrate. I see a new kind of Ghost Dance on the prairie, as increasing numbers of people take refuge in conspiracy theories and fundamentalist churches that shut their doors to the outside world. We gather in a circle and sing the holy songs that will bring back the past, that will keep at bay "their" laws and weapons and talk of dumping hazardous waste in our backyard.

Bruce Rice

The Usual Circus

in nancy's back yard grasshoppers jumping like birds
in the carragana / I stand in the shade of the trellis /
raspberry popsicle streams in my hand / bruce's kids
bill & nancy's / icecream & cake exotic ontario
cousins out on the lawn / kids doing summer*salts*
& you get down to show us how to handstand / *dad
you're76forGod'ssakestopshowingoffyou'regoingto
killyourself* / too late, 'cause there you go
legs weaving / pocketload of nickels
tumbles into air but you keep walking /
upside-down / pinwheel left / hey us kids
up there with you / marching up the blue
stairs / yelling down the green grass /
as we fall flip-flop / get back
up / sing *I'm the man who
broke the bank at Monte
Carlo* & you you laugh
so hard you finally do
fall down /

Reverend Dan Rice

Up first thing and ride
into the dust the farmyards   heat
the ship-lap porches' butter-colored
linoleum crumbling like pound cake
and endless pots of weak tea
ride all day talk
to men pulled up in fields
to a woman alone in a circle
smoothing her hands on her apron   thirty-five-pound bucket
of chop set down on a piece of its shadow

Three or quarter past
and a splash deep in the well
as I drink from a dipper
one stop for supper
then on my way
                    into the evening
the slow country cloaked in dusk as I humm
pleased
and tired as I sink into echoes
of backtrails
of childhood music hall songs
as the roses close up like footlights
as the blue planet dips
through brief shoals of aspen

Annie Bissell, Wedding Picture

I am a woman seen from a distance:
my hand neither rests
(as the photographer asked) nor does it hover
lightly
in space. I like
this picture.
This little grove suits you
a man for whom light
springs from the mind
and enters the world.
The subtle pull toward steps suggests
this is the middle of the story—
we are here to be seen
in the imagined domestic air.
As for me, I have always made my homes
on islands
full of wind
and reefs.
This could be a picture
of me sailing
from another point
of no return.

The Grandson

This family's long on memory; stories come back if they're left untold. I try to tell the one about the day Aunt Jessie picked that piece of ice out of the lake and struck my father on the head. He tells how he lay there on the bottom of the boat, sprawled across Aunt May's legs and pretending to be dead. Jessie has forgotten the whole thing. *Your father's a ham* she says *and he always acted like that anyway.* I try to make the story fit.

I can't recall actually arriving at my grandparents' cabin. I slept in a lower bunk, my face inches away from a wall of seeping logs; there were two small windows but I remember this only because I noticed them from the lawn outside. I was told my father held the plumb line as my grandfather built the stone chimney; my grandmother picked pincherries from a bush I was too small to reach or pull to the ground. My family had just arrived from B.C. in a gray Plymouth with an outside visor that curved across the top of the windshield. Eight kids in that car and I was the only one awake as my father drove, chalk-white stubble sweeping back from the headlights, a gradual yielding to bushland, to stumps reflecting our lights into uncleared pastures. The forest rolled north for miles, was larger then; the lake, I thought, was wider.

Adults came and went but the cousins spent the summer on the beach; our skin peeled and got darker. An hour after eating we lowered ourselves through vertical shade onto blazing sand and were told to avoid the whitewashed border of stones that marked a patch of thistles taller than I was. Here I come to an absence. I can't see my brother, dead now, but I know he is there swimming the lake. The boat follows, too far out for me to hear the muffling of the oars but even with my back turned I know they are there, signaling.

Regina 1987

Palest ink is better than the best memory the saying goes.

I find myself again, sitting with my father, the slats of our
lawnchairs washed in light as we watch changes in the air
above the garden. I ask about his mother. He says Annie spoke
softly to everyone except the few who trespassed on her
domain: *domain*, a word with implications but he does not
elaborate. My grandmother treated all the injuries, cuts and
sprains. She was midwife to a woman in Bengough, the only
time she tended childbirth in this country, an art prohibited
by law.

Aunt Jessie went to normal school, became a teacher and an
artist and married Frank Demaine, an elevator agent; they
cleared then sold a quarter section near Christopher Lake.
Before the war my father worked on threshing crews around
Birch Hills, the town's name said in a single breath, and he
tells how he still finds it strange to drive up that way and pass
the same fields and know there are people there who never
had to set a stook. Aunt Polly Bissell went from Scotland to
South Africa and married a man who worked for a gold mine.
That time is mostly remembered for the stories that came back
about how they were always firing the servants.

We talk through the magic hour. The grass glows softly like a
jungle illuminated from below. The signature of heat trapped
inside the high white fence is breaking down and the
conversation swings toward me, one of its anchors, gone in
the current.

Through four generations one of the men in the family has carried the name, Daniel. My father, though, has Annie's eyes. He fills the house with stories; they are stacked in rooms and closets, so many pictures of overlapping selves: the eccentric uncles; my grandfather down in a United Church basement swinging to a handstand on home-built parallel bars and teaching the boys to box; my father freezing outside the church the night of the Christmas concert. And Annie moves through it all, turning the page and shuffling the question; she is here for herself, for that which is born and cannot be called forth, this night as it pauses on the verge of speech.

West, on the Border of a Little Known County There Once Lived a Yew Tree

and everyone who lived near its shade prospered. When they came and spoke into the shade of the tree and said, "Tree, we are hungry and we haven't any bread to feed our children," the yew tree answered, "Take my lowest branch. Make it into a plow and make a furrow in the ground." The people did as the tree advised. They made the wood from the branch into a plow and when they made a furrow in the ground grain sprang up as quickly as the plow could be pulled. They made the grain into bread and when the bread was all eaten they went again and spoke into the shade of the tree.

"Yew tree," they said again, "we're hungry and we haven't any bread to feed our children."

The yew tree heard this and let its seed fall to the ground. Soon a thick forest grew up and deer and partridges came to live in the enchanted wood.

"Now," said the yew, "I have made a forest full of game. Make the wood from my lowest branch into a longbow. Use my leaves for the tips of your arrows and you will always have game on the table."

And that is exactly what they did.

One day a prince came into the forest.

"I've been hunting all day and I have killed nothing," he said to the people who lived near the yew. "Now bring me some supper and snap to it or my soldiers will kill you all."

The people were afraid of the prince so they cooked a large pot of venison as they had been ordered.

"This is the best venison I've ever tasted," he said. "I was going to kill you all, but now that I'm satisfied I think I will pay you for giving me such a good supper."

The mayor of the village was usually a prudent man, but he was so relieved their lives would be spared that he forgot himself and began to tell the prince about the astonishing tree that fed and watched over them all.

When the prince heard this he insisted on being shown the tree immediately.

"Without a doubt, this is the finest tree I've ever seen," said the prince. "You must chop it down to make a ship for my navy."

At first the people refused because they did not want to harm the tree that had been so good to them, provided their food, and was careful not to harm the children who played in its shade.

But the prince said, "If you don't do as I order, I'll tell my men to kill you all and I will cut down the tree myself."

So the people cut down the tree as they were told to. They trimmed the branches and the prince took the tree away to be made into a ship.

With the tree gone, the people were afraid the forest would die and the deer and the other animals they hunted for food would leave. But when it was noticed that the shade of the tree was there where it had always been even though the tree itself had been taken away, the people spoke into its shade as before.

"Shade," they said, "the prince made us cut down the great yew and now the forest will die and we shall all starve. What shall we do?"

"You wasted my gifts and betrayed me," the shade said solemnly, "and if not for the sake of your children, I would refuse to help you now. Tell your children to gather my branches."

The children did this and found to their surprise that when they picked up a branch they could remember everything that happened to it. The branch flexed lightly when the song of a bird that had lived in the tree ran through it; the smell of the rain rose from the heartwood; and when the children ran their fingers along the bark they heard deer breaking twigs as they walked about on the forest floor. The children kept the branches and each branch stayed fresh and green even though the child grew into an adult and then grew old and died. Then the living branches were passed on to their grandchildren and their grandchildren's children.

As long as the branch was passed on in this way, the shade of the great yew remained to protect the marvelous forest. But whenever a child grew up and left the wood or an old person who had no grandchildren died, a part of the shadow the size and shape of a branch disappeared and the forest grew smaller.

Baby Cry

Baby cry in the heart of the McMichael
Canadian Collection, unsettling as dust
on a study of flowers, a voice which calls forth
the tragic and mysteriously drowned painter
from this rich man's shrine—baby cry
and the sound from its ledges flies over Klienberg, every hilltop
wired with a hidden fence, hundred-acre hay farms and
gnarled orchards rolling down to a fen where everyday
    blackbirds
bicker like stones and cast themselves against the shadow
of an empty silo.

Baby cry in the carseat/hot/sunroof open/the stop
and start highway back to the city back to
freeways, to anxiety housing, cool wind
from the almost-come-back lake
salving the inconsolable asphalt of The Beaches condos
with their conditional desires. Baby dream, dreams
a way back to his hospital day, head crowning hairdark
as kelp at the shore: the sure doctor's hands, Mother's push and
Father coming round the end of the bed at the birthing
     moment, blood
on the toweling, baby cry
                         no saying this
                   sound, not now and not
                         ever, but ah, baby sleep
                              sleep.
                                   the arriving grandmother

          sleep.
              the daily news locked outside

                    sleep.
                         though the rainy, windy world . . .

The old house drowses, a late
migrating owl in the spruce tree calls, baby's eyes open. It is
Spring and birds arrive through the flying darkness. Over
aviation lights on twin tv towers the clear sky calls as white
impossible swans come home and the moon gleans without
     insight
the ground of last year's crop.

The family travels north to the forests of noise, camps
between lakes where "witches' broom" sways. Father's
a poet, catches what whispers, though the searching
seems futile. The right word when it's spoken, the sound
when it's said: *ah* of his pleasure, *o* of his sorrow
but hush, baby cry.

Carol Shields

Reportage

Now that a Roman arena has been discovered in southeastern Manitoba, the economy of this micro-region has been transformed. Those legendary wheat farms with their proud old family titles have gone willfully, happily, bankrupt, gone "bust" as they say in the area, and the same blond, flat-lying fields that once yielded forty bushels per acre have been turned over to tourism.

Typical is the old Orchard place off Highway 12. Last Wednesday we visited Mr. Orchard in the sunny ranch-style house he shares with his two cocker bitches, Beauty and Trude, one of them half blind, the other hard of hearing. The fir floors of the Orchard place shine with lemon wax. There are flowers in pottery vases, and the walls are covered by the collage works of his former wife, Mavis, who is said to be partly responsible for the discovery and excavation of the Roman ruins. We asked Mr. Orchard for a brief history.

"Quite early on," he mused, pouring out cups of strong Indian tea, "I became aware of a large shallow depression in the west quarter of our family farm. The depression, circular in shape like a saucer and some ninety meters across, was not so much visible to the eye as experienced by the body. Whenever I rode tractor in this area—I am speaking now of my boyhood—I anticipated, and registered, this very slight dip in the earth's surface, and then the gradual rise and recovery of level ground. We referred to this geological anomaly as Billy's Basin for reasons which I cannot now recall, although I did have an Uncle Bill on my mother's side who farmed in the area in the years before the Great War, a beard-and-twinkle sort of fellow and something of a scholar according to family legend, who was fond of sitting up late and reading by lamp light—books, newspapers, mail-order catalogs, anything the man could get his hands on. I have no doubt but that he was familiar with the great Greek and Roman civilizations, but certainly he never dreamed that the remnants of antiquity were so widely spread as to lie buried beneath our own fertile fields here in Manitoba and that his great-grandnephew, myself that is, would one day derive his living not from wheat but from guiding tours and selling postcards. Whether Uncle Bill would have scorned or blessed this turn of events I have no way of knowing, but I like to think he was not a man to turn his back on fortune."

At this point one of Mr. Orchard's dogs, Beauty, rubbed voluptuously against his trouser leg. "You will agree with me," he said, turning, "that once a thing is discovered, there's no way on earth to undiscover it."

Mavis Orchard (nee Gulching), who has been amicably separated from Mr. Orchard for the last six months, was able to fill us in on the circumstances of the actual discovery. She is an attractive, neatly dressed woman of about sixty with thick, somewhat wayward iron-gray hair and a pleasant soft-spoken manner. Smilingly, she welcomed us to her spacious mobile home outside Sandy Banks and, despite the hour, insisted on making fresh coffee and offering a plateful of homemade cinnamon-spiral rolls. Her collage work was everywhere in evidence, and centered more and more, she told us, on the metaphysics of time, and the disjunctive nature of space/matter. She is a woman with a decidedly philosophic turn of mind, but her speech is braced by an unflinching attachment to the quotidian.

"When we think of the fruits of the earth," she led off, "we tend to think of cash crops or mineral deposits. We think"—and she held up her meticulously manicured hands and ticked off a list—"of wheat. Of oil. Of phosphates. Natural gas. Even gold. Gold does occur. But the last thing we think of finding is a major historical monument of classical proportions."

At this she shrugged hyperbolically in a way that indicated her sense of the marvelous. "Arrowheads, of course, have been found in this area from early times. Also a small but unique wooden sun dial displayed now in the Morden Local History Museum, where you can also see a fine old English ax (or axe) belonging to the first settler in this region, a Mr. DeBroches. But"—and she tugged at her off-white woolen cardigan, resettling it around her rather amply formed shoulders—"when the bulldozers went into our west quarter section and came up hard against three supine Ionic columns, we knew we were on to something of import and significance, and that there could be no turning back. This earth of ours rolls and rolls through its mysterious vapors. Who would want to stop it. Not I."

Angela and Herbert Penner, whose back porch offers the best position from which to photograph the ruined arena, spoke openly to us about the changes that have overtaken their lives.

Herbert: There are problems, of course, adjusting to a new economic base.

Angela: I wish they wouldn't throw things on the ground, gum wrappers, plastic wrap from their sandwiches and so on. Last summer our family cat, Frankie, swallowed a soft drink tab and had to be taken to the vet which set us back fifty dollars if you can believe it. But most of the people who come here are just people.

Herbert: (proudly) We had visitors from all fifty states, all ten Canadian provinces plus the territories, western Europe, Japan and mainland China.

Angela: Would you like to see the guest book? One gentleman wrote recently: "Standing at the entrance to this site, one experiences a sort of humility."

Herbert: (piqued) A lady from California wrote: "Not nearly as impressive as Nimes."

Angela: That's in France. Theirs seats 20,000.

Herbert: Not the point really, though, is it?

Angela: We've managed to keep our charges reasonable. Our color film we sell at almost cost.

Herbert: (interrupting) Coffee and sandwiches is where
we make our bit of change, I'd say. Refresh-
ments. Think about that word. Re-fresh-ments.

Angela: And next year we're edging into B and B.

Herbert: Meaning bed and breakfast.

Angela: All in all we feel we've been blessed.

Herbert: (concludingly) Oh, richly, richly.

    Dr. Elizabeth Jane Harkness at the Interpretive Center replied
somewhat caustically when asked about the markings on the
stones and columns. "The motifs we find here are perhaps closer
to the cup-and-ring carvings of pre-history than to the elaborate
texts found on most traditional Roman structures," she admitted,
patting her handsome auburn hair in place, "but we find it
offensive and indeed Eurocentric to have *our* markings referred
to as 'doodles.' It is one of the great romances of consciousness
to think that language is the only form of containment and
continuity, but who nowadays really subscribes? Who? Our simple
markings here, which I personally find charming and even
poignant, are as emblematically powerful in their way as anything
the old world has to offer."
    Jay DeBroches, former grain elevator manager and great-
grandson of the first settler in the area, took us along to the
Sandy Banks beer hall, now renamed The Forum, and said very
quietly, with innate dignity, "Speaking off the record for a
moment, there was a certain amount of skepticism at first, and
although I don't like to say so, most of it came from south of
the border. It was like we-had-a-Roman-ruin-and-they-didn't sort
of thing. One guy claimed it was an elaborate hoax. A disney-
esque snow job. Like we'd done it with mirrors? Well, they sent
their big boys up here for a look-see, and one glance at this
gorgeous multi-tiered, almost perfect circle was enough to
convince them of what was what. Now we've got some kind of
international trustee set-up, and that keeps them happy, though
rumor has it they're scouring Minnesota and North Dakota with
lasergraphs looking for one of their own, but so far no luck. I

guess in my heart of hearts I hope ours is the only one. I've got the parking concession, so I'm here every morning early, and it still makes me shiver—even my fingers shiver, every little joint—when I see the dew winking off these immense old shelfy stones and giving a sense of the monolithic enterprise of that race that came before us."

The Wilfred T. Stanners family has thus far concentrated on T-shirts, felt pennants and keyrings, what Mrs. Stanners (Barb) refers to as "your takeaway trade." But she has visions of outdoor concerts, even opera. "And this place is a natural for the Globetrotters," she says, escorting us to her veranda and offering a wicker armchair.

Sal (Salvador) Petty, Chief Zoning Officer, unrolls a set of maps and flattens them on a table. We help him weigh down the edges with desktop oddments, a stapler, an onyx pen holder, a framed photograph of the arena itself during the early stages of excavation. "Here," Mr. Petty explains, pointing with the eraser end of a pencil, "is where the new highway will come. The north and south arms join here, and, as you can see, we've made allowance for state-of-the-art picnic facilities. We have a budget for landscaping, we have a budget for future planning and contingency costs and the development of human resources. None of this just happens, we made it happen."

"Speaking personally," says retired Latin teacher Ruby Webbers, "I believe it is our youth who will ultimately suffer. The planting, stooking and harvesting of grain were honorable activities in our community and gave our boys and girls a sense of buoyancy and direction. They felt bonded to the land, not indebted to it. I don't know, I just don't know. Sometimes I walk over here to the site on moist, airy evenings, just taking in the spectacle of these ancient quarried stones, how their edges sharpen under the floodlights and how they spread themselves out in wider and wider circles. Suddenly my throat feels full of bees. I want to cry. Tears, tears. Why not? Why are you looking at me like that? I grant you it's beautiful, but do beautiful monuments ever think of the lives they smash? Oh, I feel my whole body start to tremble. It shouldn't be here. It has nothing to do with us. It frightens me. You're not listening to me, are you? At times it seems to be getting even bigger and more solid and more *there.* It preens, it leers. If I could snap my fingers and make it disappear, that's what I'd do. Just snap, snap, and say, 'Vanish, you ridiculous old phantom—shoo!' "

Anne Szumigalski

The Usual Dream about One's Own Funeral

and here comes the worshipful company
driving up in dark and polished
cars, circa 1933,
rather rusted round the fenders
but still a good drive

there is my shorthair cousin
the one that works in a bank
aunts in knitted hats
my niece, my godchild
not seen since the christening
for lack of white she wears
a print of wild roses blurred
and faded by the salty air,
she sits in the highgrass
eating a sandwich
her long hair roughed
and snaggled by the wind

a pity someone forgot
I should have been sewn up
shipshape in a sail   the coffin
is green though, carapace
and plastron bossed as a turtle shell

mud to mud intones the pastor
his good boots sinking
into the shore ooze
flowers are the stunted silverweeds
with square blossoms
the color of goldfish

and oh in my girlhood
those burials at sea
a signal of dark flags
hung down between the masts
pipescreech at the sinking of the corpse
        and those memorials
for drowned sailors
when the band played
and wreaths, some of them
with lighted candles, floated
out on the swell
towards blue water

they never returned
but sometimes after a storm
I would find metal clips and hoops
beached and tangled

salt crust on the slough's lip
licked from the teeth
tasted in a strong westerly
looking out on a sea of dry grasses
bent all one way

while the pale girl
combs her snarled hair
with a comb white as fishbone
dipped in the brackish
curl of water

seas diminish, diminish
and die, as she laces
a green ribbon
through the knotted swatch of her hair

Angels

have you noticed
how they roost in trees?
not like birds
their wings fold the other way

my mother, whose eyes are clouding
gets up early to shoo them
out of her pippin tree
afraid they will let go their droppings
over the lovely olive
of the runneled bark

she keeps a broom by the door
brushes them from the branches
not too gently
go and lay eggs she admonishes

they clamber down
jump clumsily to the wet ground
while she makes clucking noises
to encourage them to the nest

does not notice how they
bow down low before her anger
each lifting a cold and rosy hand
from beneath the white feathers
raising it in greeting
blessing her and the air
as they back away into the mist

The Dove

It troubles the boy that, if you want to draw a white bird, you must use a black pencil—or, at least a dark gray one. A drawing can never get away from its hard outline.

His aunt promises him that tomorrow she will buy him black paper and white chalk, and he can try again.

"No," says the boy obstinately, "for when the sky is black it is night, and no one can see anything, not even a white bird. You can hear the whir of her wings as she passes. That is all."

"Perhaps," suggests his aunt, "it could be moonlight."

It's bedtime, and the woman places the drawing on the nightstand beside her nephew. Then she kisses him and leaves, shutting the door softly, but decisively, behind her.

The boy puts his hands over his eyes and pretends to sleep. Through his fingers he can just make out the drawing peeling itself from the page and flying away into the dark. The bird has abandoned him to his dreams.

During the long night, the child comes to the understanding that the bird is in some way his mother.

The drawing itself, he knows, is his own creature and must obey him. The bird, on the other hand, is free to follow all her whims and desires.

It is morning, and he wakes to the closed-in light of snowfall. Barefoot and tiptoe on the cold roses of the linoleum, he stares through the window. The garden and the road beyond are a single space of trackless white.

On the sill he notices a small curved feather. It could have come from his pillow of course, but maybe his aunt has placed it there, in hopes of comforting him a little for his loss.

Suspicious and grave, he takes up his crayons and gives the bird her colors: glossy yellow wings, an emerald poll, a blue breast speckled with red.

The bird is now more splendid than his mother ever was. Pinned to the paper with the brilliance of her plumage, she will never be able to escape again.

Passover

This is the burden of the solitary prisoner, eating alone like a dog at his dish. And, for lack of a companion, he is eating himself. For every man needs to share his gray hunk of bread. There he sits getting neither fatter nor thinner, and it's always Friday Dinner with no candles to light. It's always an evening in June, drawing in so very slowly towards dark.

Outside a dog is chained to the shadow of his kennel. A woman bends before him, offering an enamel plate of scraps. The dog cannot hide his disappointment; he has waited so many years for an invitation to supper. Every night he wonders, will this be the day of deliverance, when I'll sit up at the table with my paws on the white cloth, waiting for my portion, waiting for Father to fill my cup with milk.

For surely by now they have forgiven my attack on the baby, how I leapt upon her snarling and worrying. That was long ago, but still this tether is a chain of events, one leading inevitably to another, and yet one more.

But then, is it possible for a prisoner to turn his crime into triumph? Is it possible for a dog to cease longing to be a man?

The Boy at the Upstairs Window with His Head in His Hands

it is heavy as a stone he tells himself like any rock in the field
of rocks on grandfather's farm where boulders are born out of
the prairie every spring if these are the heads of huge stone
infants where are the bodies to follow narrow from shoulder to
toes after the round agony of the head or could they be
ancient skulls that the earth gives up a thousand years after
their burial what with the rain and the wind something must
surely come to light in the end for this is in many ways the
field of jesus the place where he decided to make an end of
his journey he who had traveled as far as india and back he
who has been seen in every city in the world at one time or
another just walking around stirring up trouble many times
thrown into jail for disturbing the peace of such places as this
where the bones of the earth break up and are carried away
by farmers who make piles of them in the corners of every
field and dear are these rockpiles to the child they are his
mountains and ramparts and sometimes he sees brilliant
snakes slithering in the cracks the rocks also are of every color
and grandfather says if you split one of these suckers you
could find a coiled seashell or a perfect fern or perhaps just a
hollow place the boy understands that this hollow is the very
same secret room where he lives always alone tracing the
mysterious maps on the walls with a wetted finger trying to
find how to get away from cartoons of rabbits and cats in
hero's hats to where fair ladies are advertising the subtle gifts
of the mind

Thom Tammaro

Faces at an Intersection

Fifteen billion years of cosmic history
Four-and-a-half billion years of planetary life.
Three-and-a-half million years of human history.
The whirl of atoms, the orbit of electrons,
And it all comes to this:

On a rainy afternoon in March,
At an intersection in Fargo, North Dakota,
We gather from the streets and avenues of our fates.

In the turn and strain of eyes, in the cautionary
Glances through glazed windows:
The cigarette you will never reach over to light;
The song on the radio you will never listen to together;
The turned up collar of a coat you will never reach over to
    turn down;
The discussion of the tense day at work you will never have;
The sip of gin you will never swallow in a quiet moment
    before dinner;
The meal you will never share; the loaf of fresh bread you will
    never break from the bakery where you never stopped on
    your way home;
The man or woman you will never make love to this night.

On a rainy afternoon in North Dakota,
Faces at an intersection—paused in a rainy moment—
Heading toward their lives.

Violets on Lon Halverson's Grave

> I came to this spring field to pick violets.
> But I loved this field so much I've slept here all night.
>
> —Yamabe No Akihito
> 8th century Japan

I

No one has visited you for years.
But this evening I found you at the
Far edge of the cemetery north of town,
Your headstone long toppled and cracked.
The carved letters smooth and gray to touch,
Telling me all I know of you:
"Born August 1, 1860, Norway.
Died August 1, 1892." And everything
Around you smothered in violets.

II

You did not come here to pick violets,
Nor to sleep here only for the night
Because you loved this field.
I imagine one rainy August afternoon
A few friends from your same Norwegian
Village gathered here along with the
Dutiful minister, solemn and grim, who
Dusted his hands after the gray prayer
Then walked toward town,
The prairie wide as the pastures of heaven.

III

Once in a book on wild flowers,
I read that Japanese women wove
Braids of violets to wear in their hair
To show constant love and humility
To their lovers.
And that pioneer women crushed
The velvety petals in bowls of rainwater
Gathered during prairie storms
And sipped the sweet water
To ease the pain of headaches,
Then tied bunches of fresh violets
With horse hair and placed them
In trunks, under pillows, and on
Window sills as blessings
For all around.

IV

And now I would add how under moon and stars
They grow without love, or thought, or kindness.
And how each life lived is its own orbit,
Spinning and gathering into garlands and blessings.
And that ten thousand petals and the
Shadows of ten thousand petals are unfolding
In a cemetery north of town, in the night,
As quiet and holy as the breath of God,
Fragrant and deep purple to yellow,
Spreading like pure light.

Gingko

When we were young, we gathered leaves for a big book for biology class. We dipped them in wax, pressed them with hot irons to pages and made a great book about the leaves of our region.

One, the gingko, was rare to our place. But there was a tree in front of the town bank, and some of us stole leaves at night when the wind blew through the dark, then shared them with friends the next morning. We made complete books, right books, then got A's for our leaf books.

Years later, I look for that tree when I travel home, but it is gone, gingkos gone from our region except for the leaves on our pages. In my book, I find a treeless gingko floating in its waxy world. I touch that leaf, read gingko in that book from another time.

Sometimes your life is like that: alone, detached, gone from your world. You search for a sign, a page, a leaf. Sometimes your world is like that—you're lost, listening hard for a sound, and then your memory rustles when the wind blows.

Lyrids

I

Po Li, Chinese astronomer, one April night
Six hundred years before the Christ star,
Awakened from a dream where he was
Reaching out to greet his mistress
As she drifted across the lake
On a bamboo raft.

Later, unable to sleep, he walked
From his hut out into the April night.
Resting against the trunk of a cedar,
Po Li gazed toward the heavens
And saw great sweeps of light
In the Chinese sky.
At dawn, the last bits of light gone,
He walked inside and in his notebook,
Struggling to name them, wrote
"Gliding stars," "long stars," and
"Candle flame stars" before drifting
Off to sleep.

II

Long after the lights of the town
Have been dimmed, I walk out into
The Minnesota night toward North Dakota
To watch the lyrid showers.
Earlier this evening, the local
T.V. weatherwoman said we were
Passing through sand-like particles,
All that remained of a comet
Once a mile or two wide before
It was disintegrated by the sun.
"A big dirty snowball," she called it,
And said I should be able to see
Fifteen or twenty per hour until dawn,
If I was patient.

III

Patient,
I think of lights being turned down
In a Chinese village; a man dreaming
Of his lover, reaching for her
As she drifts across the water;
A man awakening from sleep
To brush strokes of light
Sweeping the deepening dark
Of the Chinese night.

The Man Who Never Comes Back

He's always in his 60s or 70s.
A little heart trouble. Doesn't drink.
Then one day his wife or daughter or
The night shift nurse at the rest home
Comes to check on him and finds him gone.
"Was settled in for the night," they
Usually say, "in his recliner for his
Usual t.v. line-up. Never done anything
Like this before. It's not like him."
The search always begins with neighbors,
Relatives, police searching the fields
And railroad tracks near the rest home
Or mobile home court. But no luck.
This is when the local newspaper runs
The front page story with recent photo.
He was wearing a red plaid flannel shirt,
Blue winter jacket, red baseball cap.

Then the County Sheriff is called in,
And the local volunteer Rescue Squad to
Begin combing the immediate surrounding
Areas. Boy Scout troops volunteer to
Search the wooded areas on the weekend.
The river dragging comes up empty,
And the helicopter brought in from the
Local Guard yields no clues from the air.
The newspaper usually runs daily reports
And interviews with grieved family members
Who repeat he's never done anything like this.
Good news for a few days, updates, theories.
Even the local t.v. station flashes his
Picture on the evening news—a blurry shot
From a family outing a year or two ago.
Same red plaid shirt, blue coat and
Red baseball cap. There's even talk of
Bringing in a psychic from Denver.
But after a week, the updates get buried
In the back pages near the beer ads,
Good deals on used cars, and real estate.
And we're on to other news.
Years from now his name will show up in
A recent story of a man who didn't come back.
"An unsolved case," the police chief in charge
Of this new investigation will say.

But someday, I think we'll find them all.
When we least expect it. It won't be
In the fields near the mobile home court or
The wooded area along the river north of town.
We'll be out walking one evening, alone.
We'll see faint curls of smoke rising,
Hear voices echoing in the distance.
We'll follow those trails until we
Come upon the camp where all the people
Who never came back are gathered.

They'll be happy there, in their parkas and
Favorite sweaters, plaid shirts, and caps.
They'll be getting ready to settle in
To their favorite rockers, easy chairs,
And recliners for an evening of t.v.
They'll be glad to see us as they walk
Over, put out their hands to greet us,
Say, "Welcome. It's so good to see you.
You've never done anything like this before,
Have you? Well, it's ok. We've been waiting
A long time for you. We thought you'd never come."

A Photograph of You at the House of the Dead in Ascona

Far from our village on the other side of the hill, we found the
holy chancel of the Madonna della Fontana. We made
offerings, lit candles, rested in the shade of olive trees from
the afternoon heat. Later, we found the short cut—a steep
stone path—our map said would bring us to our village in half
the time and distance than the road that brought us here. And
it did.

Halfway down the hill at a "y" in the path, we found an
abandoned chapel. The tall wooden doors were faded gray
and shut tight with a rusty chain and lock. But through the
iron window bars we counted six pews and a few broken
chairs; saw red shards of votive candles scattered on a dusty
stone floor; smelled mildew and rotting boards and dank
stone. And against the altar, two crutches and metal leg braces
stood, relics of a fortunate pilgrim.

Carved in the stone at the top of the doorway a skull and crossbones and the words "La Casa della Morto"—the house of the dead—where the living come to pray. There in the mid-July heat and haze, far above Lake Maggiore, we paused in our journey down to the village, and I photographed you sitting on the steps of the house of the dead.

That night, long before the piazza cafes fell silent, we fell into bed, exhausted from our pilgrimage. But at 2:00 a.m. were awakened by the sweet voice of an Italian tenor singing opera tunes in the hotel lobby three floors below, the voice floating like an angel in the cool Swiss night, rising to our open window, then drifting above the village rooftops, beyond the bell tower of San Pietro e Paolo, into the hillsides. And we turned to each other, certain we were not dreaming the same dream—remembered our afternoon searching for the Madonna of the Fountain, descending the steep stone path, pausing at the house of the dead—so full of life and love.

Mark Vinz

Road Stop

I can't help wondering how many
times I've stayed here—nothing fancy,
the desk clerk says, clean and quiet.
So what if half the lights don't work,
the shower curtain's patched with
duct tape, a ghost convention on tv.
It's perfect, I tell her—the bible verse
right next to the ad for Tombstone pizza.

Only a few men talking weather
in the bar across the highway,
and no one I ask is from these parts.
The cool night air brings news of crops
I can't identify; beyond the ditch
the motel neon flickers but burns on.

Too late for pizza, I unplug the clock
and hide it in a dresser drawer—
another person who's not from here,
grateful for nothing fancy,
lost to the drone of semis
on the long grade out of town.

Learning to Drive

My daughter swerves, then struggles with
the wheel, jaw set. She'll get it right
next time, or maybe the next. Turns
are always hardest on these pot-holed streets,
out in the industrial park on Sunday morning.
Don't forget to signal, check the mirror
again, you'll get the hang of it—what
my father told me on some empty
country road, though he never said to
hit the brakes first, just take the wheel
and steer, make a left down at that mailbox.
I scattered gravel for two hundred feet
before we skidded toward the ditch.
Slow down, I say, and watch for ruts.
We drive in Sunday morning circles, lost
in lessons—trying to remember how
you never can predict what's out there,
not even on those routes you know the best.

Night Driving

Through patches of ground fog late at night
I think of all those childhood trips I had
to sleep on someone's couch. Houses, faces,
even parents disappear—only the chairs
remain, straight-backed chairs to keep me
from rolling out. But there are hands, too,
gentle ones that smooth the sheets and fluff
the pillows of my nest, and through the
cracks of light come grownup voices murmuring.
Who can say what we really remember,
what stays lost? Beneath me, four thin
tires whine on curving, hilly roads
between the misty walls of grass and trees.
And here and there in my headlights
are the eyes, hesitating, waiting to come out.

Driver Education

I must have been the only boy
in junior high who didn't know
a camshaft from a universal joint.
Even my friend Charlie read the
hot-rod magazines, dreamed his
mother's '56 Bel Air would someday
be a car worth cruising Lake Street in—
with a little work, you know, some
pin stripes and those rumbly pipes.
We'd learn how to lower the rear end,
too, and find something cool
to hang from the rearview mirror.

I had to admit it would be great
to have a car like that—to have it,
not to make it. Even Charlie
thought I must be nuts—
me, with my father's old '48 Ford
sitting out in the garage unused.
There, in that dim light we'd test
those strange pedals. Clutch,
he'd say. You've got to push it
down to change the gears.
What did I care about shifting
when there were stale cigars in the
glove compartment? Just let me
light one up, I'd say—with matches
I'd stolen from my mother's box above
the stove—then you can teach me gears.

He'd watch my smiles turn green
and there we'd sit, shifting and
puffing through our Saturdays.
You'll never learn to drive that way,
my friend kept reminding me, and
for those moments he was the crazy one.
Then he'd tell me to put it out. I'm
getting tired of this, he'd say. Besides,
I've still got to show you how to steer,
how to keep your stupid eyes
on the road ahead.

The Other Side

Hoods were the ones who knew
about wheels, who smoked and shaved
and even got the stuck-up girls
to turn their heads.
Like Kenny Liston in his black
leather jacket and motorcycle boots
with those half-moon cleats, years
older than the rest of us 9th graders,
who said he kept a switchblade
somewhere up his sleeve. Kenny Liston
under the awning of the little store
across the street, chain-smoking Camels
while we watched amazed from the
windows of our history classroom.
Kenny Liston, begging my English
homework and getting it, because
it never hurt to have a friend like him
who kept the others off you in the pool.
Kenny Liston in typing class
the day the teacher said he was
hopeless, always jamming the keys.
We watched his throat and ears
turn red, and then he did it—
took the brand-new Smith Corona
to the third floor window and
pitched it out.
                    Later, we heard
Kenny robbed the little store and shot
it out with cops over on Clinton Avenue.
The rumors grew. He'd stolen a
beer truck and passed out samples
at Central High just up the street.
He'd taken the principal's car and
driven all the way to Florida. Who

knows the truth in 9th grade anyway?
All we cared about was that he
terrified us, that he knew what
we didn't and dared to do it.
How we hoped we could forget Kenny,
never imagining we'd be meeting him
over and over again, out there
cruising in his stolen wheels with a
back seat full of smashed typewriters,
giving the finger to all the hopeless cases
trapped behind the window glass.

Handy Man

You'd think he'd know my car by now, but every time I bring it in—which lately has been just about every week—I have to tell him all over again.

"It's the '84, right?" he says.

"No, it's the '83, the one you said needed to have the brakes bled."

"Brake line," he says. "You don't bleed brakes." And then he launches into this long explanation about rotors and pads, just like he did last time about the pump that was shot—water or gas, I can't remember which.

Darrell's Auto Service has me again. And if Darrell can't fix it at his own shop, then he always has a friend who can. Mickey's Auto Air. Dave the Muffler Man. Roy's Auto Body. They all go by their first names, real chummy. At least they don't call themselves an auto service, like Darrell does. Makes it seem like he's some kind of philanthropist, which is an enormous joke.

Ellen says I should think about taking a course in basic auto mechanics at the tech school. That's her answer to everything. She takes courses all the time—sewing, gardening, interior decorating, you name it. But who's going to put bread on the table when I'm taking courses? That's what I keep asking *her*.

It doesn't stop with the car either. Since we live in an older home there's always something that needs fixing. That's when my so-called friend Rodney shows up. He too has an answer to everything.

"It's really simple," Rodney says, like I'm a total failure as a human being if I can't understand him. "You don't want to pay someone to do *that*," he keeps telling me, no matter what it is. Like replastering the ceilings, which are falling down in pieces all around us. Like putting in a new garage door after Ellen backed through it. Like fixing the leaky pipes in the basement, or the huge cracks opening in the driveway after all the rain we've been having. There aren't enough courses at the tech school to teach me all I need to know just to live in my own house, and Rodney thinks it's obscene to pay someone to do what any homeowner should know how to do. "Not hard to be handy," is Rodney's motto.

It's not just Rodney either. All my neighbors are like him. They reshingle their roofs and rewire their kitchens. All of them have basement workshops full of equipment they're always trying to loan me. They've got books, too, even videotapes. And they all love to go to the hardware store. If I ever have to go to the hardware store after work or on Saturday, I'm sure to see at least a couple of my neighbors there. They want me to ooh and aah over their new power saws and socket wrench sets. More than once I've had to buy a bunch of screws or nails just to throw them off the track. I've got a big box of that assorted junk in the basement, and the only time I ever use any of it is if Ellen wants me to hang a picture or something. But I haven't even done that lately. The last time I tried to put in a nail I ripped a big hole in the living room wall. So aside from something really major, if anything around the house needs fixing I just try to ignore it and hope that one day soon I'll be making enough to move us into a new house. The car's another matter, though. I need it for my work, so here I am talking to Darrell again. I think he must cover himself with grease even when he's not working, just to show people he's a mechanic. Like Rodney says, you can always tell who's handy and who's not just by looking at him.

"Take a little longer'n I thought to get the parts," Darrell is telling me. "That was an '84, wasn't it?"

The walls of Darrell's shop are covered with auto parts and tool posters and calendars, every one of which seems to picture a scantily clad girl holding up some piece of equipment or sitting on an enormous motorcycle. It's after pacing around awhile when all those beauties start to close in on me that I head across the street for a cup of coffee at The Pantry.

"We've been seeing a lot of each other lately," I kid Millie, the waitress, when she comes to my booth near the door.

"Got the old car blues again?" she says. "I sure know what it's like, but who can afford a new one?"

"Who can afford anything?" I say, and we both laugh. Talking to Millie always makes me feel better.

"Well, I've got some good news for you," she says. "We've got this fantastic boysenberry pie today and I've been saving the last piece for someone special. I guess you're him."

I realize that Millie reminds me a little of those women on Darrell's walls. I can't help it. She's got this long black hair she's just had permed.

"Look like a million today," I tell her when she brings the pie and refills my coffee. I mean it, too. Like a million bucks. Then she glances around the cafe, which is nearly deserted, and she slides in across from me.

"What's old Darrell up to today?" she asks, lighting a cigarette.

"Bleeding the brakes—brake lines, I mean."

"Don't know much about brakes," she says. "Know how to bleed a radiator, though. Harold showed me just before he left."

"Sounds impressive." I can't help wondering how Millie would look on a motorcycle.

"Sorry," she says. "Harold's my ex. Sure was nice having him around for as long as it lasted, but I can't say I miss picking up after him."

Last week when I was here, she told me about her oral surgery. Once she gets to know you a little, Millie's not one to hold back—or worry much about business. One of the guys from the lumberyard down the street is heading toward the cash register, but Millie doesn't make a move to get up. I can tell he's from the lumberyard because he's wearing a big tape measure on his belt. He just looks over at us and shrugs, then throws a couple of bills on the counter and leaves. There's only one other guy in the place, and he's reading a newspaper.

"Harold was good to have around for one thing," Millie says and winks.

"Oh?" I say, trying not to show that she's surprised me. "And what might that be?" I like the way she draws in the cigarette smoke from her mouth to her nostrils. We used to call it "frenching" when I was a kid, but I haven't seen anyone do it in years.

"He was good for fixing things," she says. "Handy Hal. That's what I used to call him. You good at fixing things?"

"I can change a light bulb," I say, and she laughs.

"You're a great kidder."

"Well, I have done a little plumbing repair," I say, which is the truth—sort of. Not long ago I spent an entire afternoon trying to get my mother's toilet to stop running all the time. I even went to the hardware store and got one of those litle rubber flappers, which seemed to do the trick. My mother kept going on about how impressed she was with her son, the plumber, but about a month later Ellen finally told me she had to call a plumber for my mother the very next day because I'd put the whole thing in backwards. Good old Mom hadn't wanted to hurt my feelings.

"You should come over to my place some time," Millie is saying. "I bet there are some things you know how to fix real good."

"As long as it's not your car," I say, and we both laugh again. "I couldn't even change the oil."

"Go on," she says. "If Harold could show me how to change oil, it can't be all that hard. Everybody knows how to change oil. You're some kidder."

Millie has to go and pick up onion rings for the man reading the paper, so I throw a five on the table and slip out in a hurry. Some kidder, all right.

When I get back to the shop and look for Darrell, his feet are sticking out from under the front end of my car, which he's got propped up with hydraulic jacks.

"Be done under here in a few minutes," Darrell tells me, "but I thought I should tell you that you need some new struts, too. Leaking pretty bad. Couldn't see it till I got under here. You want to get down here and see what I mean?"

"That's okay," I say. "Sounds like it might be serious."

Darrell's voice is getting fainter under the car. "You bet," he says. "Better get at these next week. You got some time next week?"

"I'll have to let you know," I say, fishing in my pockets for a quarter before I realize I can use the phone on Darrell's counter, right below the picture of the bathing beauty wearing a little mechanic's cap. "Let me check with my wife."

When Ellen answers, I can hear her perfectly, but for some reason she can't hear me. "Hello?" she keeps saying. "Who *is* this?"

So I'm talking louder and louder into Darrell's grimy receiver, just to say not to worry, that I'll be home pretty soon.

"Tell her about these struts," Darrell says from under the car, and I can barely hear him now. "I wouldn't let *my* wife drive with struts like these."

"Is that you?" Ellen keeps asking. "Is that you?"

"Who do you think it is?" I tell the receiver. I don't think I can get much louder.

The smiling beauty on Darrell's wall clock is pointing her wrench toward five o'clock.

"Umph mumph wumph," Darrell says from under the car.

"I just wanted to let you know I'm coming home," I'm screaming.

"Who is this?" Ellen says. "Is this some kind of joke?"

Will Weaver

Pets, Inc.

Constance Dickerson, thirty-four, became engaged to one of her students, Shawn Halvorsen, twenty. Connie, a tall, haphazardly dressed woman with brown hair pulled back in a loose ponytail that showed an occasional strand of gray, was an instructor of English at the university. Shawn, a sturdy blond fellow from a dairy farm near New Ulm, was a General Studies major who had managed to miss freshman English until spring quarter of his senior year, when the university computer directed him to Connie's Comp 101 class.

Semicolon trouble sent him to her office soon enough.

"If they're pretty much interchangeable," Shawn said, "then why couldn't I use periods instead of semicolons?" He asked this of Connie with an earnest, encouraging smile; he had wide, white teeth. "For the rest of my life, I mean."

Connie took three personal leave days. It had been a long year of short essays, and illiteracy she could take but cheerful illiteracy was another matter.

And besides, her cat was dying.

Katmandu, a brown and white Siamese male with a narrow face, had been with Constance through the B.A., the M.A. and the Ph.D. Now Kat was fifteen years old. In the past six months he had grown as skinny as the silverfish he used to bat about the bathtub, and in the past six weeks Connie had spent over $480 at the veterinarian's.

First there was kidney failure; this required intravenous treatments of the renal system, along with twice-daily doses of pink liquid Omoxycillin. Then there was the pulmonary edema; for this poor Kat took injections of diuretics, which required Connie to fashion for him small diapers made from small adult Depend undergarments and masking tape. To keep up his strength Connie fed Kat with a large eye-dropper a liquid nutrition formula that smelled and looked a lot like curdled cream; the appearance of the eye-dropper produced Kat's sole energetic movement of the day—a leap behind the couch. And now there were heart problems, arrhythmia and low blood pressure, for which Kat took small white tablets to dilate the blood vessels, improve the flow.

Despite such heroic measures, Katmandu seemed smaller every day. He was shrinking away to a sad, homely little smile. On the most recent visit, the veterinarian had given Connie a little cardboard wheel chart that translated animal (aardvark through zebra) years into the human life span. "Try to see it this way," he said, "Katmandu is ninety-nine years old."

During her three days off, Connie remained in her apartment with the shades pulled, Katmandu sleeping beside her bed on a little rubber sheet, she in her robe. Alternately she looked through old photos of Katmandu, read Sylvia Plath and called out for pizza. A small, leaning tower of pizza cardboards rose on her nightstand. When it finally tipped onto the floor she spent an afternoon staring down at platters, at their greasy swirls. She came to think they contained some kind of message. A text. A text, which, with deconstruction, would provide a signal of hope for Katmandu and/or American public university education. She sniffled. A large tear fell, beaded up on the cardboard.

In the middle of this belly-dragging, mud-wallowing foolishness her mailbox lid clanked. She sat up and blinked, wiped her eyes. In the post she found a single, cheerful letter:

"Heres hoping, that your feeling better."
Shawn Halvorsen

Three errors within seven words. She returned to class the next day. And there was Shawn Halvorsen, third row center.

"Feeling better, Miss Dickerson?" he said immediately as she entered the room.

"Ms," she said.

"Ms," he said pleasantly.

Several students turned their heads to stare at Shawn. One girl, Cindy, who wore a silver crew cut and a small gold pin in one nostril, rolled her eyes and groaned.

"I am better, thank you, Mr. Halvorsen," Connie said. And that day, because she had no lesson plan she assigned in-class essay number three, "A Distressing (Sad) Personal Experience from Which I Learned an Important Lesson."

The students all set to work, all except Shawn Halvorsen. He sat staring down at his paper with the pink end of his tongue clamped between his teeth, fidgeting his feet, putting one leather shoe atop the other, his cheeks ripening with color like tomatoes in June, until the bell rang. The other students dropped their essays on the table and hurried off; when they were all gone he approached Connie's desk.

"Yes, Mr. Halvorsen?"

"This sounds strange, maybe," he said, "but I'm fairly certain nothing sad has ever happened to me."

Connie glanced briefly at the wall clock. "A death in the nuclear family," she said, and began to sort the essays into alphabetical order.

"No," Shawn said, "knock wood!"

Connie did so at once—and immediately felt cheap for being manipulated—in particular by a male at least ten years her junior.

"Death in the extended family?"

Shawn paused a moment. "No."

"Death of classmates." She moved through D's to E's.

"Nope," he said, "our class was real lucky that way."

"Dead neighbors."

Shawn squinted briefly. "Mr. Johannson lost both legs in a tractor accident."

"Dead pets." Connie suddenly looked up from her papers and in the same instant crushed someone's essay between her hands.

Shawn stared. At her face. At the crumpled pages. "Hey—are you okay?"

Connie began to iron the essay with a slightly trembling hand.

"Certainly," she said. "I was, I was asking you about former pets, ones that might have . . . passed away."

"Once I had a 4-H heifer that was struck by lightning."

"And killed?"

"Right now—you bet," he said, and made a small clapping motion with his hands.

"Didn't that . . . stir you, make you sad?"

"I suppose. A little."

"All that work, that closeness to an animal, certainly there was some feeling of loss, some early insight, some sense of fatalism, a brush with the existential?"

Shawn stared at her. He scratched his head. "Maybe I was lucky in a way. She was struck by lightning the day after the county fair. I'd already gotten the purple ribbon and she was sold anyway."

"Sold?"

"That's part of cattle showing. When the judging is over you have to sell your heifer to the highest bidder."

Connie looked up. "Why, that's terrible!"

"It's, well, always been that way," Shawn said, his voice a trifle puzzled. He thought a moment. "I guess on the farm, animals come and animals go."

Connie thought again of Katmandu, undoubtedly hungry by now, his diaper in need of attention. She glanced at the clock. "A high school sweetheart then," she said briskly, professionally.

"Some of them, yes," Shawn said. His cheeks colored slightly.

"But I suppose sweethearts come and sweethearts go?"

"I guess so." Shawn's face shaded a deeper red.

As he looked down, Connie stared at him for a long moment during which she imagined his girlfriends. Plump blondes. Cheerleader types with puffy hair in front and banana clips in back. But into sight as well came darker, taller, homelier, thinner, Honor Society types who stood behind the blondes, looking over the tops of the fuzzy yellow geysers of hair, watching him pass down the hall, watching him catch the football, watching him carry his tray through the cafeteria—homely girls too shy to wave or to ever come forward, content to be heartbroken from a distance.

"Well, write on something cheerful, then," Connie said suddenly and with surprising sharpness, "your life certainly seems to have plenty of cheerfulness in it."

When she left the classroom Shawn Halvorsen was waiting in the hallway.

"I'm sorry, Miss Dickerson," he said, "I didn't mean to bother you."

"No matter. That's what the university pays me for," she said. She kept walking.

He followed her.

"Though not for being crabby," she said, glancing up with a brief smile. "It's late and I guess I'm hungry."

Shawn nodded.

They walked through the doors and into the spring afternoon. It was five o'clock already on the university mall; beneath the canopy of tall elm trees, twilight drooped.

Shawn stopped abruptly. "I know—" he said, "I'll call my folks, tonight, and I'll ask them if anything sad has ever happened to me."

She paused to stare up at him. She found herself waiting for some kind of punch line. The joke of it all. The clever closure to which university conversations aspired.

"So what do you think?" Shawn smiled down at her, his breath warm and sweet in the cool air.

Her eyes dropped to his mouth, to his square chin, then traveled back up to his blue eyes, then dropped again to his mouth, to the wide whiteness of his teeth. Something inside her fluttered.

She stepped backward—nearly stumbled. She swallowed—felt the flutter again. Then, as if outside her own body she heard herself say, "Mr. Halvorsen, would you like to get a pizza or something?"

"With you?" he said excitedly.

✦ ✦ ✦

"Tell me his major again?" Connie's father said. Her parents had flown immediately from Baltimore to Minneapolis when they heard news of the engagement. The three of them sat at Stub's Pizza Pub; Shawn had gone home to the farm for the weekend. Connie's father, a trim, white-haired man who developed computer programs for the Treasury Department, chewed on the stem of his straight, unlit briar pipe with a rapid clattering sound. Her mother, a smaller version of Connie, folded and refolded her napkin that by now was coming apart at the creases.

"General College," Constance said.

"That means he can teach?" her father said.

"Not yet."

"He does have plans?" her mother said, attempting a smile.

"He's not sure."

"Business? *Small* business?" her father said.

"Frank, please—" her mother said quickly. Turning to Connie she said, "His parents do have a farm, don't they?"

"Yes."

"Farms are like businesses nowadays, aren't they?"

"Not theirs," Connie said to her mother. "Theirs is only 160 acres and rather old-fashioned. Shawn much prefers city living."

Her parents exchanged sidelong glances.

"How will he support you?" Frank asked.

"Father—*I* have a job, remember?" Constance said rather sharply.

"But not tenure," her mother added.

Connie shrugged slightly.

"So that's just it," her father said. "What will *he* do?"

Constance looked out the window. A red car passed.

"Connie, honey, what skills does he have?" her mother asked. "Is he good at any one thing?"

As she stared out the window a slow, moony look came onto Connie's face, and she turned toward her mother and could only grin.

"Really, Constance," her mother said, looking away, beginning to twist the napkin pieces into tiny ropes.

"Job skills!" her father thundered. "Things he could make a living at!"

"Well," Constance said. She thought a few moments, then a good deal longer. Finally she said, "He's naturally cheerful?"

After seeing her parents off at the airport, her mother red-eyed and sniffling, her father pipeless because he had bitten through and crushed its stem, Connie hurried back to her apartment to check on Katmandu. Nowadays he did not stir from his box, not even for the eye-dropper.

Recently, Shawn, in a cheerful and encouraging way, had brought up the unthinkable. Connie had burst into tears. Of course she knew it was the right, the only humane thing, but how could she? How could anyone?

Her apartment door was unlocked. Shawn, who had a key, lay on the couch reading a Louis L'Amour novel.

"I thought you went home this weekend," Connie said.

"Well, I did, but just to get some things," he said. He sat up.

She noticed by the doorway a small, somewhat battered Sears tool box, a roll of gray duct tape, a carefully folded piece of black plastic.

"Katmandu?" Connie said, shrugging off her coat, "did you do his diaper?"

"Well, yes and no," Shawn said. He stood up.

Connie paused—froze—one arm still in her jacket sleeve.

Shawn came across the living room and put his hands on the sides of her shoulders. "Katmandu is happier now," Shawn said slowly, gravely, "he's in a better place."

"No!" Connie cried. She swooned.

After Connie revived, Shawn led her out through the patio door into the small backyard. There, beside the tulip bed was a tidy, rock-covered mound brightened by freshly cut dandelions. She swooned again.

Later, at Pizza Chuck's, they ate in silence. The end of the CBS evening news was on, a light-hearted piece about the George Bush family of black and white spaniels. Millie and her brood. As she watched the dogs cavort on the White House lawn Connie again broke into tears. Shawn wiped her cheeks with his napkin, refilled her glass with Bud.

"How did you—I mean what did you use?" Connie blurted.

"Use?" he said blankly.

"You know!"

Shawn pushed a piece of black olive-anchovy her way. "In times like this it's important to eat," he said.

Her eyes fell to the black olives. Shawn's gaze returned to the TV, to the news. There President Bush hoisted two pups by the napes of their necks, a gesture which resulted in 286 letters from across the country instructing the president on how to lift animals safely and kindly.

✦ ✦ ✦

Once a week Connie shared a bag lunch with several sister professors whose solidarity came from their similar teaching contracts: fixed-term, non-tenure track, one year renewable. She told them about Shawn and Katmandu.

"Sicko!" said Cheryl from the Psych Department. "Dump him—today—that one's real trouble."

"Obviously some kind of domination move," agreed Gail from Anthropology.

"Not necessarily," said Sue from Sociology. "Something had to be done, and you couldn't do it on your own, right?"

They all turned to Connie.

She looked down, ashamed.

Quickly they all crowded around in a protective circle and sang the chorus from Joni Mitchell's song, "The Circle Game."

During dessert of double fudge brownies, Cheryl from Psych said to no one in particular, "My dog, Taffee. Bob's never liked her."

"We see," the group said gravely and in unison—after which they giggled.

"Especially nowadays," added Cheryl, who did not laugh. She looked away, out the window. "I had Taffee long before I met Bob. She was used to sleeping on the bed."

The listeners looked furtively at each other, waggled their eyebrows.

"I just shooed her off," Cheryl said. "But now, well, she's fourteen years old and her hind legs are kind of paralyzed."

"Kind of paralyzed?" said Gail.

"So she sleeps on your bed?" said Sue.

Cheryl from Psych looked down at her hands.

"Like all night?" Gail added.

"Where on the bed?" asked Sue.

"Not between you, certainly?" said Connie.

The psychologist turned to face the group and smiled wanly.

"Cheryl honey, there's somethin' strange in your neighborhood," said Sue.

"So who you gonna call?" someone said.

In mid-giggle all of them, slowly, turned to look at Connie.

Connie stared back at them. Her eyes widened.

Cheryl-the-psychologist's husband, Bob, an attorney, was so grateful to be done with Taffee that, when it was over, he slipped a fifty-dollar bill into Shawn Halvorsen's pocket.

"Really, it was no trouble," Shawn protested. He stood in the doorway with an old, oversize suitcase hanging heavily from one arm, his small Sears tool box from the other.

"Cost me twice that much at the vet's," Bob said. "And besides, you have your expenses, your overhead." His eyes dropped briefly to the suitcase.

"Only three dollars at Goodwill," Shawn said, lifting the suitcase for Bob to examine.

Bob waved off his objections and slid past Shawn to the front door. "Fifty bucks for peace of mind?" Bob said, showing Shawn out. "Everyone should be so lucky as me, right?"

✦ ✦ ✦

Lawyers are not without friends, nor do they lack an eye for value. Within two days Shawn received four calls for his "services," as the callers phrased it. On the phone they spoke in long, somewhat elusive metaphors about the "general quality" of their lives, about the "erosion of certain freedoms," of "situations in need of resolution." For Shawn, it was hard to tell what they wanted or even if they had the right phone number.

He began to interrupt them. "You have a pet you want me to take care of?"

"Exactly," they said.

The first caller, a periodicals librarian, had an incorrigible Manx cat. The woman left a key for Shawn in the mailbox, along with fifty dollars and a bottle of 1968 Mirassou Cabernet Sauvignon.

The second call concerned a rheumy-eyed spaniel owned by the English Department chairman who had only two days earlier left for Scotland on a year-long Fulbright. His wife was the caller. "Will you be home when I come?" Shawn asked.

"Are you kidding?" the woman said with a high, cackling laugh. "I'm going to mix myself a Manhattan and pull up a chair."

The third call concerned a large, clumsy, pure white and purebred Alaskan Husky that belonged to a young woman music professor who was moving to Berkeley. Shawn took a liking to the big mutt, kept him in his dorm room for three days while he did some phone work, and soon enough placed the dog on a farm for a ten-dollar profit.

Emergency calls paid better. American Tabby cat would not ride in the cab nor in the rear of a twenty-four-foot U-Haul truck; when Shawn arrived, the man and his wife were standing braced against opposite sides of the truck, their arms folded. The cat sat high atop the cab like a fat orange hood ornament. The kids screamed. The neighbors stood framed in their windows. Shawn drove the whole family down the street to the Dairy Queen, and while they were eating their Blizzards, he slipped out a side door and took care of business.

✦ ✦ ✦

Shawn soon enough had little time for his studies. His phone rang with regularity. Pleasant service, affordable prices—within six weeks he had to install an answering machine in his dorm room. In three months he set up an office in the warehouse district and hired two part-time men, optimistic young lads from farms near LaVerne and Alexandria. They interned with Shawn twenty hours a week while they majored in Animal Science; they were happy with the work, and said the internship looked great on their resumés.

That following spring Connie, due to university retrenchment, was cut to half-time, but by then she and Shawn were married, and she spent much of her time with PETS, INC. Her contribution, having "been there," as she put it, was to develop a Separation and Grieving Service. This included, for the worst-case clients, personal counseling along with memoir-writing as therapy (on a correspondence basis). In most cases an extended phone call or two did the trick, and in all cases the customer received a card of condolence for which Connie wrote original sonnets, sometimes Petrarchan, sometimes Shakespearean, with approachable sentiments about the arrival and eventual passing of pets.

Shawn seldom went out on calls anymore, so busy was he with the office and the records. Help was needed. Connie's father, following a most generous offer from his son-in-law, moved to Minnesota to join the firm where he took over the business and accounting end of things. This allowed Shawn to work on the franchising of PETS, INC.

Traveling much of the week, he quickly established new franchises in New York and Los Angeles, and then in Atlanta and New Haven and Denver.

At the end of the first year, Shawn, with his father-in-law's help, took PETS, INC. public. An initial offering of one hundred thousand shares soared eighty percent in value the first week, and *Fortune* and *World News Report* both called Shawn a "new breed" of American entrepreneur. Shawn was voted "Young Business Person of the Year" and was brought to the White

House Rose Garden to receive personal congratulations from President George Bush.

✦ ✦ ✦

On the White House grounds it was a bright sunny April day. The black and white spaniels, nearly full-sized now, raced twice through the crowd, causing a good deal of hilarity—even the president had to wait until they were shooed away—but finally the remarks began.

"I've brought Shawn Halvorsen here today," the president said, "because he pretty well sums up my vision of America. First, in this great country of ours it pays to be cheerful."

Applause.

"Second, in this great land of ours there are still all kinds of ways to make a buck."

Laughter and sustained applause.

In the photo opportunity that followed, President Bush was observed to speak privately and somewhat intensely, close observers thought, with Shawn Halvorsen. Afterward, they turned to face the crowd and the cameras. The next day, photographs in most national newspapers showed the president and Shawn smiling, and the president, as is his habit, pointing cheerfully into the crowd. Only one photographer, from *Mother Jones* magazine, captured the truth of the moment.

President Bush, it could be seen, was pointing not at the crowd but beyond it—to the horse-shoe pit—where four of the black and white spaniels, sand showering behind them, were madly digging out one of the stakes. Beside the president, his eyes fastened on the dogs, Shawn Halvorsen smiled his cheerful smile.

Dave Williamson

Retrieving

Bob Jenkins, high school principal, dabbler in the stock market, husband, father of two grown-up kids, owner of an overly affectionate golden retriever, wakes early one Saturday morning in February to find no one beside him in the queen-sized double bed. He remembers that his wife Barb is away this weekend; she's down in Grand Forks, North Dakota, with some of her women friends, curling and shopping.

This is Barb's idea of a treat, to be away with other women, drinking scotch, telling raunchy jokes, playing bridge in her nightie. She says she's going to buy some clothes while she's down there, but she's not going to smuggle anything across the border. Her friends can lie to the Customs officers if they want to, but Barb's going to declare everything and pay the duty.

Jenkins wonders, Should he get up or should he stay in bed? It's wonderful to have a choice, and the decision is an easy one to make: he'll get up and enjoy the tranquility—cook his own breakfast, walk the dog, settle down to read for as long as he wants.

He sits up, swings his legs out from under the covers and heads for the shower. This activity does not arouse Dave, the golden retriever, who sleeps on his own duvet on the floor. The family named him Dave out of some quirky desire to be unique; when they purchased him just over four years ago, the breeder said that one name he'd never heard anyone give a dog was Dave. Dave knows Jenkins is going to be a while in the bathroom so there's no point in getting up yet.

In the kitchen a little later, Jenkins, in purple dressing gown, raps an egg sharply on the edge of the frying pan, holds the split egg over the salted boiling water and parts the halves, letting the syrupy insides drool into the pan as he ceremoniously lifts the shell to a great height so that his arms form an arch. The gesture seems almost religious, a benediction on what is surely going to be a grand breakfast. The coffee's on, the two slices of whole wheat bread are in the toaster, the water in the pan is coming to a boil. He opens the refrigerator and takes out a tub of margarine; for the ten-thousandth time he worries about the "g" in "margarine" being soft even though it's followed by an "a." He pours some freshly squeezed orange juice into a glass and takes a sip. Ahhh! It's great to be alive, cooking your own breakfast on a Saturday morning.

He hears a bark that tells him Dave is up and wanting out. Jenkins ignores Dave for the moment because the egg is ready. He butters his toast, lifts the egg out and flops it onto one of the two slices. He takes his breakfast to the kitchen table, sprinkles pepper and salt on the egg and dashes to the back door to let Dave out into the snow-covered yard. Dave sniffs the air then runs out, dives nose-first into the snow and rolls over onto his back. He squirms this way and that, all four feet in the air, giving his back a good rub. Jenkins swears there's a smile on Dave's face.

At last, Jenkins can sit down and read the Saturday newspaper while he eats his breakfast. He cuts into the egg. Ahh—done just the way he likes it—a little soft in the center but not runny. He tells himself he could probably cook an omelet and bake an apple pie if he really wanted to.

Jenkins turns to the sports pages and the article on the game the hometown Jets won last night over Edmonton. He'd been at the game as the guest of his neighbor, Tom Leggett, and—

The telephone rings. He fully expects it to be Barb, checking in with some new gossip or a run-down on what she's bought so far at Columbia Mall. He'll have to be careful not to forget to ask how they're doing in the curling.

"Hello?" says Jenkins.

"Hi, Dad."

It isn't Barb, it's Tracy, his twenty-two-year-old daughter. Jenkins senses a problem because Tracy usually opens a phone conversation with "Bonjer."

"How're you doing?" he asks, suspecting that she might be having trouble with her two roommates.

"Great," she says. "Thought I might come over to see you this morning."

"You know your mother's away—"

"Yup. I want to see *you*. Okay if I come over?"

"Sure. But what's up?"

"Can't I tell you when I see you?"

"Of course. If I'm not here when you get here, I'll be over in the park with Dave."

After he's hung up the phone, he pours himself a cup of coffee and spreads some strawberry jam on a slice of toast. His Saturday morning solitude has been spoiled. Or has it? Perhaps Tracy wants his advice—she's been talking about getting out of her job as secretary in a housing developer's office. Maybe she wants to tell him something *good*.

Sounds of water upstairs tell him Brian's up and having a shower. Brian, his twenty-four-year-old son, still lives at home and seldom gets up before 10:30 any morning. He's an actor who works part-time at a video store called Movie Madness. Jenkins checks the time: 9:26. Brian must have to go to work. Has he just now turned on the shower or was he in there for a couple of minutes before Jenkins noticed? Brian has the bad habit of staying in the shower till the hot water turns cold.

Dave barks at the back door. By the time Jenkins gets there, Dave is leaping high in the air, hoping someone will notice him. Jenkins lets the dog in and Dave rushes straight over to a cupboard door to sit and stare at it. The dog seems to believe that staring at the cupboard door will open it and magically cause a Milk Bone cookie to descend into his ever-expectant chops. Jenkins thinks, As long as I'm the only one soft-hearted enough to give him a cookie, he won't get too many; but Jenkins knows the whole family thinks this way. No wonder Dave is fat.

The shower is still running.

Jenkins heads upstairs thinking, Maybe Tracy wants to move back home. Hope for this springs eternal. Jenkins and his wife have told Tracy that, if she comes home and goes to university, they not only won't charge her room and board, they'll pay her tuition. Jenkins opens a dresser drawer to take out his long underwear. The sound of the drawer brings Dave tearing upstairs. This is a reflex action that would warm Pavlov's heart: sound of opening drawer means Dave's master is about to get ready to take him for a walk. Dave pants, barks, runs back and forth, salivates at the thought of all those lovely smells he's going to be sniffing. Jenkins wishes he could make his wife this happy this easily. He dons the underwear, a warm shirt, a heavy sweater and his cords. He tucks his pant-legs into an extra pair of wool socks.

The shower is still running.

Enough is enough. Jenkins's watch tells him it's 9:43. Brian's been in the shower for at least seventeen minutes. Jenkins is sure that, despite their many discussions of the subject and the number of times he has shown Brian the quarterly bill and the moving numbers on the water meter, Brian still thinks water is free in Canada. Jenkins pounds on the bathroom door.

Brian is not one of those people who sing in the shower. Though he has a reasonable tenor voice and has been known to perform well in singing parts, he uses a shower for rehearsing his impersonations. The last time Jenkins knocked, he was answered by W.C. Fields: "Pray, what is the nature of your business, my little chickadee?" This time, it's John Cleese: "Oh, blahst, is that you, Sibyl? Is everything all right, then, dear?"

The water continues to run.

"Brian, *we're running out of water!*"

Now Clark Gable as Rhett Butler: "Frankly, my dear, I don't give a damn."

But the flow of water does stop. And Don Adams as Maxwell Smart says, "Sorry about that, Chief." Relieved, Jenkins heads downstairs. Dave sits at the door doing his best imitation of an obedient dog. He has fetched the leash from the back hall and it lies at his feet as he sits there panting in anticipation. Jenkins puts on his toque, his scarf, his parka, his snowboots and his fleece-lined mitts. Just before he heads out, he goes to the answering machine to turn it on in case Barb phones and Brian is pre-occupied. He remembers how much Barb hates to hear her own voice ("Hello. You've reached the Jenkins residence. We aren't here right now . . ."), so he decides not to set the machine. Instead, he calls upstairs, "Brian! Your mother might phone, so answer it if it rings, will you?"

Humphrey Bogart answers: "You betcha, shweetheart."

Telling himself he's done all he can do, Jenkins hooks Dave up to the leash and leads him out.

It's still overcast; in fact, snow is falling. At least there is no wind. Large flakes are coming down, covering the mud that's left over from the last thaw. Jenkins takes a deep breath and then another. He loves winter walks in the crisp air when the wind isn't raging. He continues to breathe deeply while his dog sniffs at rabbit tracks here, a patch of urine there. One of Dave's bad habits is to pick up used Kleenexes and chew them. When he does this, Jenkins usually seizes the dog's jaws and attempts to pry them apart to pull out the soggy tissue. Today, when they come upon a used Kleenex in the street, Jenkins is alert enough to yank Dave's head up just before the dog can get his teeth into it.

At the entrance to the park is a large sign recently erected by the city. It says: DOGS MUST BE KEPT ON LEASH. DOGS MUST NOT BE ALLOWED TO DEFECATE IN PARK. ALL DOG DROPPINGS MUST BE PICKED UP BY OWNER IMMEDIATELY. As a law-abiding citizen, Jenkins obeys almost all signs. He does allow himself one act of defiance and this he carries out now: right beneath the sign he unhooks the leash from Dave's collar. Dave dashes off, following rabbit tracks into a dense bush. Jenkins always expects a police car to drive by while Dave is romping free. He has his speech ready for the moment he is apprehended: "See these tire tracks? See these broken beer bottles? Why don't you catch the people who did *this?*"

Of course, Jenkins would feel a little more confident about letting Dave go if the dog were fully trained. He and Barb took Dave to puppy school and failed. Maybe they were too impatient or too soft-hearted; they couldn't get Dave to heel and sit and stay on command. Now they fervently believe that Dave's winning personality is a result of his not being obedient.

As he walks along through the snow, enticing Dave to follow by giving him cookies at regular intervals, Jenkins sees a rusty old

Datsun come into view. It's over on the street that runs adjacent to the park and the driver is waving. It's Tracy. She parks the car (Tracy calls it "The Beater") and gets out. Jenkins stops walking to wait for her. Dave stops sniffing, notices someone approaching, sits and points his nose in her direction. It's always difficult to tell which he picks up first, the sight or the scent. But he definitely recognizes her. He scampers over to meet her.

"Dave, come *here!*" Jenkins calls, but it's a futile cry. Occasionally, Dave does come when called, but only, it seems, when he's trying to get on the good side of Jenkins, or when there's absolutely nothing to distract him. At this moment, Tracy is a major distraction. The dog has always gone crazy over her. The theory is that, when they brought him home from the breeder, Tracy was the first to feed him.

Tracy stops to brace herself on the snow-covered ground, about halfway between her car and her father. Dave runs so hard, he actually goes past her, then abruptly stops, the way dogs do in movie cartoons, and nearly loses his balance. He quickly recovers and leaps toward her. He squeals—the sound is one of ecstasy, perhaps even orgasm—he's so happy to see her.

"Hello, Dave, hi, Dave, come on, Dave, it's okay, fella, it's okay, yes." Tracy's patter sounds more like a catcher talking to a moody pitcher than a young woman talking to a dog. "Easy, now, Dave, easy—no! Give me that!"

Dave has hold of her mitt. Tracy tugs at it, realizes a tug-of-war might ruin it and lets Dave have it. Dave romps away—it's playtime.

"Daddy," says Tracy, "can you get my mitt?"

For a moment, Jenkins feels good; it isn't often these days that anyone in the family defers to him as the one who has the answers or the expertise. He feels a surge of confidence that he can rescue the mitt.

"*Dave,*" he says in a sharp, stern voice, "give me that mitt."

The dog is glad to have the full attention of two of his favorite people. He vigorously wags his tail. Jenkins dives for the mitt. Dave jumps away. At times like this, Jenkins swears that the dog is mocking him.

Tracy watches patiently. She's pulled her mittless hand inside the sleeve of her ski jacket.

"Okay," says Jenkins, "you stand right there, Trace. Get ready to grab him when I count to three. One . . . two . . . three!" He lunges; Dave bounds in the opposite direction and runs into Tracy. He's blocked just long enough for Jenkins to get hold of his collar. "Give me that mitt!" He seizes the dog's jaws and yanks them apart. The mitt falls free.

"Thanks, Dad," says Tracy, scooping it up.

"These dogs are bred for hunting," says Jenkins. "Can you imagine trying to get a bird away from him?"

"Oh, *gross!*" says Tracy. "My mitt's got *gob* all over it. That's all I need." She wipes it off in the snow.

Having had his fun with the humans, Dave runs away, sniffing for traces of other animals.

"So what's new, Trace?" Jenkins dares to ask.

His daughter tosses her long brown hair off her face and shakes twice as if she's suddenly cold. She rubs her ears with the mitt that's still dry. When, Jenkins wonders, do girls finally acknowledge that maybe you should wear something on your head in winter?

"I've been wanting to talk to you guys about this, but everybody's always so busy," she says. Her voice seems a little shaky.

"We'll always make time to talk when you have something on your mind, Tracy, you know that."

"I know, but it isn't always easy to get started on some of these things. I was thinking maybe Bill should be with me."

Oh, oh, thinks Jenkins, this *is* serious. It involves Bill, the guy she's been seeing for more than a year. Can she be pregnant? What an old-fashioned thought! She *can't* be—Tracy is a pragmatist who knew about birth control before she hit puberty. Has Bill given her an engagement ring? Jenkins saw her bare left hand when Dave had the mitt—was there a ring on her finger?

"Dad, the guy who's been living with Bill is moving down east. Bill wants me to move in with him."

For a fleeting second, Jenkins thinks she said Bill wants her to move in with the guy who's moving down east. He quickly realizes it's a question of ambiguity in the pronoun "him," and she's telling him, Jenkins, that he, Bill, wants her to move into his, Bill's, place with him, Bill.

"We think it'll be a good idea from, like, an economical standpoint," says Tracy. "The rent's five hundred a month and I'm paying two hundred now, so I'll just be paying fifty more, and I'll be able to get away from Trish and Dana, who've been sort of getting on my nerves lately."

Jenkins notices that, in this explanation which has been blurted out all in a rush, there's a suggestion that she's getting a bargain despite her having to pay out fifty dollars more a month, and there's a declaration that her two roommates are suddenly a pain after being the perfect friends from the first day Tracy wanted to leave home. What has been left unsaid is that good old Bill is not only going to be able to stay in the same place at no increase in rent, he's also going to get all the sex he wants without having to leave his apartment. As they say in the Chrysler commercials, *Advantage: Bill.* Jenkins wonders why there's been no mention of *love* in this.

"Dave!" Jenkins yells. "Come and get a cookie!"

To his surprise, the dog stops chewing on a branch and comes right over to get his Milk Bone. There are times when Jenkins thinks he thinks his *name* is Cookie. That's he, the dog, not Jenkins or Bill.

"Well, Daddy," says Tracy. "What do you think?"

"First, let me say, I'm glad you're discussing this *before* you move in with him. Uh—you *haven't* moved in with him yet, have you?"

"*Daddy.* Of course I haven't."

"Okay. Well, like I say, it's good of you to ask us what we think before you do this. Now, I know you think your mother and I are old-fashioned, but you know what we've always said: If you choose to set up house with some guy, you're going to be closing a few doors . . ."

Tracy's pleasant young face grows ugly with anger.

"Daddy, I'm not setting up house with 'some guy,' I'm setting up house with *Bill.* And if you mean by closing doors that we wouldn't be welcome in your house—"

"Trace, I'm talking about doors of opportunity. You know how much we want you to get more education—"

"Living with Bill won't stop me from going to university if I want to! God, I thought it was just *Mom* who thought like that—"

"Oh ho! So your game is divide and conquer, is it? Get dear old Dad on his own and he'll agree to anything. Well, I—"

Jenkins stops speaking not only because someone else has entered the park but because that person—a man—has a German Shepherd with him and Dave has seen them.

"Now, Dave," Jenkins says, "you *stay*, there's a good boy."

Dave does stay, sitting a few feet from Jenkins and Tracy, closely watching the man and the dog advance toward them. They seem to be following the path that's been worn through the middle of the park and, if they continue that way, they will pass by a few yards from Dave. To avoid any possible skirmish, especially since this man has his dog on a leash, Jenkins thinks he'd better get Dave on *his* leash. After all, the sign does say DOGS MUST BE KEPT ON LEASH. The man's wearing one of those woolen balaclavas and Jenkins can't see much of his face but he can tell from his walk that he's a no-nonsense type. He's holding his leash just so and the German Shepherd is walking just so on the man's left in the perfect heel position. Jenkins wants—quietly, without any fuss—to slip the hook of the leash onto the ring of Dave's choke collar.

"So that's your answer, is it?" says Tracy in a challenging way. "You're *against* Bill and I—"

Dave takes off. Dave, who seldom barks, barks. If he'd stayed a split second longer, Jenkins would've had the leash on him. Now Dave is running straight toward the man and the German Shepherd. Jenkins runs after him, trying to seem nonchalant, the consummate dog-owner. Dave bounds around the other dog, wanting it to play.

"*Dave*," Jenkins says. He grabs for the collar, misses, gets a handful of Dave's mane. He hangs on as best he can but he falls to the ground, hauling the damned disobedient cur down with him. "Sorry, sorry," Jenkins says, red-faced, as his shoulder hits the crusty snow. "I am sorry about this." All his self-respect is gone.

The man doesn't speak. The German Shepherd doesn't utter

a sound. The two of them look disdainfully down at Jenkins and his unruly beast as they continue on their way.

"Daddy, I'm *going,*" says Tracy, who is already hurrying off toward her car.

Jenkins wonders if this is *it*—is he losing her?

"Tracy," he calls, "wait, be reasonable—"

"I'm not *leaving,*" she calls back. "I have to get into the car. I'm *freezing.*"

Dave squirms out of his master's grasp and runs after Tracy. Jenkins sits up in the snow and watches them hurry away from him. He's still holding onto his end of the leash.

Biographical Notes

David Arnason teaches at the University of Manitoba in Winnipeg. He has written stage plays; scripts for film, radio and television; and several collections of poetry and short stories. His latest book is a collection of short stories called *The Happiest Man in the World*.

Ven Begamudré was born in South India and he moved to Canada at the age of six. He is the author of *Sacrifices*, a novella, and *A Planet of Eccentrics*, a short story collection, and co-editor of an anthology, *Out of Place: Stories and Poems*, with Judith Krause. He lives in Regina, Saskatchewan.

Ron Block was a Minnesota Voices Project winner in 1988 for his book-length narrative poem, *Dismal River*. He currently lives in Fargo, North Dakota, where he writes fiction and poetry and teaches at North Dakota State University.

Carol Bly's work has appeared in *The New Yorker, The New York Times Book Review, Best American Stories* and *The Norton Reader*. Her collections include both essays—*Letters from the Country* and *Bad Government and Silly Literature*—and short stories—*Backbone* and *The Tomcat's Wife*. She divides her time between Sturgeon Lake and St. Paul, Minnesota.

Di Brandt is a writer, teacher and editor who lives in Winnipeg with her two daughters. Her first book of poetry, *questions i asked my mother*, was nominated for Canada's Governor General's Award and won the Gerald Lampert Award. Her second book, *Agnes in the sky*, won the McNally Robinson Award for Manitoba Book of the Year, 1990.

Bonnie Burnard won the 1989 Commonwealth Best First Book Award for her first collection of short stories, *Women of Influence*. Her stories have appeared in the anthologies *Soho Square III* and *Canadian Short Stories*. She lives in Regina.

Sharon Butala is the author of five novels, *The Fourth Archangel*, *Upstream*, *Luna*, *The Gates of the Sun* and *Country of the Heart*, and two collections of short stories, *Fever* and *Queen of the Headaches*. She lives on a ranch in southwest Saskatchewan near the town of Eastend.

Dennis Cooley was born and raised in Estevan, Saskatchewan. He is a poet and professor whose works include *Bloody Jack* and *Perishable Light*, poetry, and a collection of critical essays, *The Vernacular Muse*. A former president of the Manitoba Writers' Guild, he lives in Winnipeg.

Lorna Crozier is the author of seven books of poetry, the last two of which, *The Garden Going On without Us* and *Angels of Flesh, Angels of Silence*, were both nominated for Canada's Governor General's Award. She lives in Saskatoon, Saskatchewan, but most recently taught writing at the University of Victoria, B.C.

Alan Davis, a native of Louisiana, has taught at Moorhead State University in Moorhead, Minnesota, since 1984. He is the founding editor of *American Fiction*, an annual anthology of short stories. In 1991, he was a winner of the New Rivers Press Minnesota Voices Project competition with a story collection, *Rumors from the Lost World*.

David Allan Evans has published three volumes of poetry, *Hanging Out with the Crows*, *Real and False Alarms* and *Train Windows*, and a collection of autobiographical essays, *Remembering the Soos*. He teaches in the English Department of South Dakota State University in Brookings, South Dakota.

Linda Hasselstrom lives and works on a cattle ranch in western South Dakota. Her books include *Windbreak: A Woman Rancher on the Northern Plains*, a year-long journal, and *Going Over East*, essays. In 1990, she was named Author of the Year by the South Dakota Hall of Fame. She seldom goes anywhere without her dog and her handgun.

Bill Holm was born and still lives in Minneota, Minnesota, when he isn't teaching or traveling in places like Iceland and China. His four books are *Boxelder Bug Variations*, *The Music of Failure*, *Coming Home Crazy* and *The Dead Get By with Everything*. He sometimes teaches at Southwest State University in Marshall, Minnesota.

Robert King is a professor of Creative Writing in the English Department at University of North Dakota in Grand Forks and co-director of the UND Writers' Conference. His two chapbooks of poetry are *Standing Around Outside* and *A Circle of Land.*

Robert Kroetsch won the 1969 Governor General's Award for Fiction for his novel *The Studhorse Man.* He has published several works of poetry, such as *The Complete Field Notes*, and his other novels include *But We Are Exiles, The Words of My Roaring, Gone Indian, Badlands, What the Crow Said* and *Alibi.* He lives in Winnipeg.

Jay Meek has published five books of poetry, most recently *Stations* and *Windows.* He currently directs the writing program at the University of North Dakota in Grand Forks, is co-director of the UND Writers' Conference and poetry editor of *North Dakota Quarterly.*

Kathleen Norris lives in Lemmon, South Dakota, where she's had a "crazy-quilt" of jobs, such as business manager for a family farm and instructor at a continuing education center for clergy. Her poetry books include *The Middle of the World, The Year of Common Things* and *How I Came to Drink My Grandmother's Piano.*

Bruce Rice's poetry has appeared in many magazines and anthologies. His first collection, *Daniel,* won the 1989 Canadian Authors Association Award for Poetry. He lives in Regina.

Carol Shields was born in Oak Park, Illinois, and moved to Canada in 1957. She lives in Winnipeg, where she teaches at the University of Manitoba and writes fiction. Her two collections of short stories are *Various Miracles* and *The Orange Fish.* Her latest novel—her sixth—is *The Republic of Love.*

Anne Szumigalski has published eleven books, most recently a collection of poetry called *Rapture of the Deep.* In 1989, she was awarded the Saskatchewan Order of Merit. She lives in Saskatoon.

Thom Tammaro was born and raised in Pennsylvania. Since 1983, he has taught writing and humanities at Moorhead State University in Moorhead, Minnesota. He has edited various books and is the author of *Minnesota Suite,* a chapbook of poems.

Mark Vinz is the author of several books of poetry, the most recent of which are *Mixed Blessings* and *Late Night Calls.* His short fiction has appeared in several magazines and in newspapers via five PEN Syndicated Fiction awards. He teaches at Moorhead State University in Moorhead.

Will Weaver lives in Bemidji, Minnesota, where he teaches writing at Bemidji State University. His novel, *Red Earth, White Earth,* was developed for TV and broadcast by CBS as a two-hour special. His collection of short stories, *A Gravestone Made of Wheat,* won the 1989 Minnesota Book Award.

Dave Williamson writes book reviews for the *Winnipeg Free Press* and other journals. He is the author of several short stories and TV plays and three novels: *The Bad Life, Shandy* and *Running Out.* Dean of Business and Applied Arts at Red River Community College in Winnipeg, he will be Chair of The Writers' Union of Canada for 1992-93.

About the Cover Artist

Timothy Ray was born in Indian Head, Saskatchewan. He grew up in Regina and studied art at the universities of Manitoba and Arkansas. He currently teaches at Moorhead State University. His work has been shown in many cities, with solo exhibitions in Winnipeg, Fargo/Moorhead and Grand Forks.

Acknowledgements

DAVID ARNASON: "The Star Dollars," "Me and Alec Went Fishing with Rimbaud" and "Lamb's Lettuce" printed by permission of the author. VEN BEGAMUDRÉ: "Sand Dollars" by Ven Begamudré reprinted from *A Planet of Eccentrics* by permission of the publisher, Oolichan Books. RON BLOCK: "Abandoned Farmstead," "Messenger," "A Warning," "Lunch," "Death of the Jaybird," "The Power Plant" and "Down in the dump, some tires burnin'" are selections from *Dismal River: A Narrative Poem* (Minneapolis: New Rivers Press, 1990). Reprinted by permission of publisher and author. CAROL BLY: "Male Initiation: An Ancient, Stupid Practice" printed by permission of the author. DI BRANDT: "completely seduced," "the day my sister left us," "trees are not enough," "last night i became" and "that day, when i became" will be published in *mother, not mother*, a collection of poems by Di Brandt, Mercury Press (September 1992). Printed here by permission of the author. BONNIE BURNARD: "Figurines" printed by permission of the author. SHARON BUTALA: "Absences" and "Things Fall Apart" printed by permission of the author. DENNIS COOLEY: "small light from our window," "that's it then isn't it," "me holding your hand holding back," "a certain muskiness a numbness," "never planned it this way," "the morning after," "don't you see philip don't you see," "by the gosh i just waltzed him," "look he says look at this" and "& you do you look up" printed by permission of the author. LORNA CROZIER: "Living Day by Day" first published in *Canadian Literature*. "Canada Day Parade" first published in *Grain*. "Cleaning Fish" first published in *Prairie Fire*. These poems and "Inventing the Hawk," "Country School" and "On the Seventh Day" will be published in *Inventing the Hawk* (McClelland and Stewart, Spring 1992). Reprinted here by permission of the author. ALAN DAVIS: "Growing Wings" first published in *Pulpsmith* (Spring 1982). Reprinted by permission of the author. DAVID ALLAN EVANS: "The Pond," © 1991, printed by permission of the author. LINDA HASSELSTROM: "Coyote Laughs" and "Following a Cabin Cruiser in a Blizzard" printed by permission of the author. "Prairie Relief" and "Pennies for Luck" first published in *Land Circle: Writings Collected from the Land* (Fulcrum, Inc.: Golden, Colorado, 1991) and reprinted by permission of author and publisher. BILL HOLM: The first half of "Glad Poverty" first published in different form in *Unexpected Fictions* (Turnstone Press, 1989). Reprinted by permission of the author. ROBERT KING: "In the Northern Towns," "Old Lake Agassiz," "Late Harvesting" and "At Reevey's Prairie" reprinted by permission of Dacotah Territory Press. "The Car at the Edge of the Woods" reprinted by permission of *North Dakota Quarterly*. "The Girl in Valentine, Nebraska," "Walking with Father in Colorado" and "How I Get Home Tonight" printed by permission of the author. ROBERT KROETSCH: "The Cow in the Quicksand and How I(t) Got Out" first published in *Border Crossings*. Reprinted by permission of the author. JAY MEEK: "Surprising Nights," "Walking the Mall," "North from Deadwood," "Postcard from the Center of the Continent," "Friends and Neighbors Day," "Cries," "Out" and "In Charge of Laughter" printed by permission of the author. KATHLEEN NORRIS: "The Sky Is Full of Blue & Full of the Mind of God" first published in *Prairie Schooner*, Summer 1989 (University of Nebraska Press). © Kathleen Norris. Reprinted by permission of the author. "Dakota: Or, Gambling, Garbage, and the New Ghost Dance" printed by permission of the author. BRUCE RICE: "The Usual Circus," "Reverend Dan Rice," "Annie Bissell, Wedding Picture," "The Grandson," "Regina 1987" and "West, on the Border of a Little Known County There Once Lived a Yew Tree" reprinted from *Daniel* (Cormorant Books) by permission of the publisher. "Baby Cry" printed by permission of the author. CAROL SHIELDS: "Reportage" first published in *Prairie Fire*. Reprinted by permission of the author. ANNE SZUMIGALSKI: "The Dove," "Passover" and "The Boy at the Upstairs Window with His Head in His Hands" reprinted with permission from *Rapture of the Deep* (Coteau Books, 1991). "The Usual Dream about One's Own Funeral" and "Angels" printed by permission of the author. THOM TAMMARO: "Faces at an Intersection" and "Violets on Lon Halverson's Grave" published in *South Dakota Review* and in *Minnesota Suite* (Spoon River Poetry Press, 1986). Reprinted by permission. "Gingko" first published in *College Composition and Communication* (National Council of Teachers of English, 1991). Reprinted by permission of author and publisher. "Lyrids" published in *Midwest Quarterly* and in *Minnesota Suite*. Reprinted by permission. "The Man Who Never Comes Back" first published in *North Dakota Quarterly*. Reprinted by permission. "A

Photograph of You at the House of the Dead in Ascona" first published in *University of Windsor Review*. Reprinted by permission. MARK VINZ: "Road Stop" first published in *North Dakota Quarterly*. Reprinted by permission of the publisher. "Learning to Drive," "Night Driving," "Driver Education," "The Other Side" and "Handy Man" printed by permission of the author. WILL WEAVER: "Pets, Inc." printed by permission of the author. DAVE WILLIAMSON: "Retrieving" printed by permission of the author.